EVELINE MAHYÈRE

(1925-1957) was born in Geneva, her mother was a schoolteacher and her father a bank manager. Although from a Protestant family she was sent to a convent after her expulsion from the Voltaire Lycée in Geneva, where she returned to take her *Maturité*. Eveline Mahyère then went to Paris, winning a scholarship to study for a year in Madrid. Returning to Paris she took a degree in Spanish at the Sorbonne, and began work as a translator. She translated whodunnits from English into French, and worked for the publishers Stock. In 1955 she translated Alberto Denti di Pirajno's *A Cure For Serpents*; they became close friends.

Throughout her life Eveline Mahyère was subject to depression. After the first bad bout in 1950 she convalesced for some months in Dartmouth where her older brother had a teaching post at the Royal Naval College. *I Will Not Serve*, her only novel, a small autobiographical masterpiece, was written shortly before she committed suicide at the age of thirty-two. Published as *Je Jure de M'Eblouir*, in France it was instantly recognised as a work of considerable distinction. This edition was translated by Antonia White—author of the *Frost in May* quartet and translator of Colette—and published in 1959.

I WILL
NOT SERVE

EVELINE MAHYÈRE

Translated by
ANTONIA WHITE

With a new introduction by
GEORGINA HAMMICK

Virago

Published by VIRAGO PRESS Limited 1984
41 William IV Street, London WC2N 4DB

First published by Editions Buchet-Chastel, Paris, 1958, under the title
Je Jure de M'Eblouir

First published in Great Britain by Frederick Muller Ltd, 1959
Virago edition offset from Frederick Muller 1959 edition

British Library Cataloguing in Publication Data
Mahyère Eveline
  I will not serve.—(Virago modern classics)
  I. Title   II. Je jure de m'eblouir,
  English
  843'.914 [F]   PQ2625.A/
  ISBN 0-86068-306-0

Printed in Great Britain by
The Anchor Press at Tiptree, Essex

"Why, up to now, have I never been able to love people unless I substituted them for God? Where did I get this mania? Doubtless from my craving that God would at last reply. Exhausted by my monologue, I created God on earth and launched frantically into a dialogue. Is it surprising that so much sublimity soon became ridiculous?"

Sylvie's Journal

INTRODUCTION

If the seventeen-year-old heroine, or perhaps more correctly anti-heroine, of this novel were all-of-a-piece she would have less appeal and less conviction. In Sylvie Ceyvenole, Eveline Mahyère has drawn a complex and intriguing character whose personality and life are composed of paradoxes. She is an unbeliever who sees God as her rival, a rebel who has given her heart to a member of the establishment. Resolutely anti-life, her crusade is to prevent Julienne Blessner—in Sylvie's eyes the embodiment of the Virgin Mary—from choosing the living death of the convent. Yet when there is a real chance—by embracing Julienne Blessner—of achieving her aim, Sylvie can't take it:

> A worshipper cannot bring himself to blaspheme; I remained petrified, vanquished. She did not belong to me; she belonged to Sainte-Thérèse, under the blue mantle of the Blessed Virgin, on an invisible pedestal that removed her from me. How could I do anything but kneel? Should I have loved her if she'd been the kind of woman one takes in one's arms?

Sylvie's dilemma is that the possible has no appeal. It is the desire for the impossible that both fires and destroys her.

Mahyère is subtle in allowing Sylvie's idealised Julienne Blessner credibility while at the same time letting us see her as a human being with ordinary failings. If there is evidence of the "quiet courage" the pupil admires in the teacher, we see another side when Mlle Blessner tries to offload the problem of Sylvie and her *Baccalauréate* onto her (Mlle Blessner's) own model, Mother Marie Sainte-Cécile. And is it courage, or fear of failing in a profession (of architecture), then as now dominated by men, that has made Julienne Blessner give up her career for the convent? Again it seems, if not hypocritical, inconsistent of her to insist on Sylvie passing her "*Bac*" when she herself has opted out of her studies just before taking her degree. Sylvie at least sits her exams, and her "Loneliness of the Long Distance Runner" tactics—whereby she proves to herself that she can pass in all subjects including the despised mathematics (another traditionally male-dominated subject) and then, resisting the temptation of a paper on Baudelaire that's right up her street, deliberately fails in her best subject French—although foolish, show an independence of spirit and toughness of resolve of which one suspects Julienne Blessner to be incapable. (I say "suspects" because Mahyère the narrator makes no judgments and never tells us what to think.) This lack of authorial interference means that we don't know what Julienne Blessner, the inspirer of a formidable and obsessive passion, looks like. Sylvie, who throughout the book is talking to herself and not to us, never describes her. Julienne's eyes—it is eyes, after all, which according to tradition reflect the soul—are perhaps the key:

> There is something that you have never told me, something I've been able to read in your look when, twenty times in a single lesson, our eyes used to meet over the little plaster statues. It is because of that look that I've left the convent.

A few pages later, Sylvie confides in her diary:

> I no longer wish for hell. In any case, isn't it heaven that I love in Julienne (unless it's the colour of her eyes).

The image of her eyes recurs forcefully throughout the book, as, for instance, in Sylvie's saying: "the desire for your eyes scorches me so", in which we are reminded that whereas for English readers Julienne Blessner's name contains a benediction, in its original—via *blesser*—it implies a religious wounding. Towards the end of the novel we get Claude Ceyvenole's impression of Julienne. As Sylvie's cousin and confidant, he has heard a great deal about her, and though prepared to admire her mental gifts he has already decided that Eleonore (Sylvie's private name for Mlle Blessner) is probably, at twenty-five, a "rigid, rather pathetic old maid". When he does meet her he is too busy, in his role of confirmed atheist and defender of Sylvie trying to get a rise out of Julienne, to notice much about her appearance. All we learn is: "Claude regretted that Julienne did not strike him as being remotely desirable." Contrasted with Sylvie's

impassioned ravings, this flat observation is an
indirect comment on the blindness of love.

When the novel opens, the key event, Sylvie's
expulsion from the Convent of Sainte-Thérèse-de-
l'Enfant Jésu, has already taken place. We are
propelled into the drama by Sylvie's theatrical letter
to her former teacher. Mahyère uses the opening
paragraphs partly as a device for scene-setting (it
must be for our benefit that Mlle Blessner is told facts
she already knows), but by the end Sylvie's authentic
voice comes through. Letters—Sylvie's to Julienne
Blessner and to her cousin Claude; Mlle Blessner's
long-awaited and unsatisfactory replies, and her own
to Mother Marie Sainte-Cécile; Claude's to Sylvie,
etc.—are central to the book. The story unfolds
through them and through Sylvie's by turn ecstatic
and despairing confidences in her diary. Linking
these is the narrator who chronicles events and
Sylvie's emotions in a voice that is quiet, sympathetic,
amused—but detached. It's a voice that reflects the
"example of detachment and love" that is Julienne
Blessner's ideal, but which for Sylvie is a meaningless
paradox.

I first read *I Will Not Serve* in 1959, the year Antonia
White's translation was published in England. I don't
remember what made me buy the book (an arresting
jacket? My copy has long since lost the one it must
have owned) but I do remember the impact it had on
me at nineteen, my curiosity about its author—of

whom I knew nothing more than brief facts of her death given in André Bay's preface—and my frustration on discovering there was no more Mahyère to read. I know I was impressed by her strong, uncluttered prose, and by its aphoristic quality—a sententiousness, in the purest sense, which did not seem then, and does not now, to degenerate into platitudes—and there are pencilled underlinings of examples of this throughout my copy of the book.

What could a passer-by do—come to her aid, take her to hospital? No charitable soul could have understood the absence of Julienne. People pity a man who falls from scaffolding, a woman who loses her husband. Because they suffer? No, only because they have the official right to suffer.

There are people in whom, even when we see them every day, we only dare confide on paper.

At seventeen only one expulsion seems fatal: expulsion from love.

It is not God I hate: it is the use His faithful make of Him.

It may not be fair to remove these examples from their contexts, but they do typify the French idiom, accent and reference of the whole. Sylvie's precocity, articulate intelligence, self-mockery, worldliness— above all, her extravagance—are foreign to the English, to whom reticence and discretion are virtues (in England, to wear one's cleverness on one's sleeve is a crime), and her life in Paris—familiar to us from the novels of Sagan—has no real equivalent in the

London of the 1940s-50s. Middle-class schoolgirls then, however rebellious, drank *cappuccinos* in coffee bars, not whisky in pubs. (A glass of "medium" sherry was the most they could expect to be offered at home.) Whisky is part of the seventeen-year-old Sylvie's rebellion—she has convinced herself that most drunkards are mystics—and she gets through a great deal of it in the course of the book. Even Julienne Blessner, preparing to "die to the world" has no difficulty in knocking back the gin fizzes, and one is reminded that alcoholism in France was already enough of a national problem to warrant a government campaign. Ubiquitous posters encouraged: *Santé et Sobriété* or warned: *L'Alcool Tue*.

Whisky being a spirit, it can also be seen as a symbol of the fire and intoxication of love in a book that is plaited with religious metaphors—some obvious ("a mist was softening the sky, the mist threw a halo round the trees"), some less so (Julienne Blessner, as I've said, was training to be an *architect*). Mahyère, by her use of contrast, points up the contradictions in Sylvie's character. People and place all have their counterpart: Sylvie/Albine; Julienne/Claude; Claude/Francois; Saint-Thérèse/L'Ecole de Beaux Arts and the Racine Bar; the Luxembourg Gardens/ the Cemetery of Montparnasse. Similarly, the Ceyvenole parents—Protestant, austere, vegetarian —are compared with the liberal and hospitable family of her best friend Albine de Cêtres. If Sylvie feels at home anywhere it is with them, but her profound feelings of alienation—an extreme version of what many adolescents suffer—permeate the book:

> But suddenly I became conscious again of this emptiness inside me, all round me; this scorching absence. I feel myself at the furthest end of time and distance.

It was this absence of a reason for living that drove Eveline Mahyère to her suicide, and *I Will Not Serve*, like many first novels, contains strong elements of autobiography. The guise of fiction allowed her to explore different aspects of her own personality at different ages, so that if, in all essentials, Sylvie is the adolescent Eveline, Claude—"this Diogenes who lived in garrets, who by his refusal of life placed himself outside life in a falsely Satanic universe"— must in part be Mahyère ten years on. The narrator too is her own older and—despite the flashes of sardonic humour—sadder, refracting voice. The background details are certainly based on Mahyère's own, whose parents, like Sylvie's, were Protestant. She was close to her mother, an energetic and devoted schoolteacher whose Christianity in the words of Eveline's brother Jean "was sincere, profound and real". Again, like Sylvie, Mahyère was expelled from a Lycée (in Geneva) and sent to a convent school—Mon Séjour, at Aigle. (The Lycée agreed to take her back when, the nuns no longer able to cope with her defiant nonconformity, she was about to be expelled a second time, and it was from the Lycée that she took her *Maturité*, the Swiss equivalent of the *"Bac".)*

Even while seeing her as a ruthless sentry at the walls of an order and a religion that keep her and Julienne Blessner apart, Sylvie in the novel admires and cannot help liking Mother Marie Sainte-Cécile. She may well be drawn from a nun, Mother Marie Sainte-Clotilde, who played an important role in Mahyère's schooldays at Mon Séjour, and with whom she remained in contact all her life. Mother Marie Sainte-Clotilde thought highly of Mahyère's intelligence and literary ability, as, later, did M. Bouchardy, respected and feared as one of the best French teachers of his day, when he taught her at the College Voltaire.

Sylvie's gift for friendship, and her estimation of its value as being above that of love, reflect Mahyère's own. At school Eveline's *copains* were always among the most interesting and original pupils. Friends in her adult life, often writers, included the eccentric and secretive E.M. Cioran who described Mahyère as "a sort of female Rimbaud", and Maurice Bardèche and his wife Suzanne (a sister of Robert Brasillach). Eveline and her brother spent a part of each summer holiday staying with the Bardèches at their house in Carnet-Plage in the eastern Pyrenees.

In Rome in 1955 she met Alberto Denti di Pirajno, best known to English readers for *A Cure For Serpents*, a book she was then translating into French. Not knowing Italian, she worked from the English text (it seems a waste, incidentally, that Mahyère's Spanish, in which she took a degree at the Sorbonne, following a year's scholarship at the University of Madrid, proved useless to her as a translator, since French publishers almost invariably required her to translate English and American authors), and she became very friendly with di Pirajno who helped her to restore in the French the passages considered too shocking by the English translator. Already an old man when they met, di Pirajno nearly died of a heart attack not long afterwards, while climbing the four flights of stairs to her flat in the Rue Saint-Louis en l'Ile where he was due to dine with her.

Eveline's best friend, *confidante* and mentor was her elder brother Jean, to whom I am indebted for this brief biography. They shared friends, holidays and books, together discussing the "five greats of the epoch": Proust, Gide, Valéry, Claudel and Ramuz. Also Brasillach, Giraudoux, Apollinaire and de Montherlant. (When Sylvie quotes de Montherlant to Julienne Blessner—"Et la gent fémino-chrétienne bat des ailes en criant l'amour, l'amour"—and Julienne is nonplussed, it confirms our suspicion that the pupil, as well-versed in Saint Augustine as in Baudelaire, is smarter and brighter than the teacher.)

Eveline Mahyère turned to her brother in all her troubles, and he had the importance, if not the character, in her life that Claude has in Sylvie's. It was to him she went to convalesce in 1950 after a serious bout of the depression that dogged her life, staying for several months in Dartmouth, where Jean Mahyère held a teaching post at the Royal Naval College. (Several years earlier she had stayed with him at Frensham Heights School, near Farnham, where he also taught French.)

I am not sure if Eveline Mahyère enjoyed her job as translator. Getting her work in on time was always a drama, and the pep pills she took (the drug corydrane Sylvie uses when working for her "*Bac*" and later takes an overdose of) were as destructive in the long term as they were helpful in the short. Nevertheless, André Bay, her editor at Stock, thought highly of her work and said so in his preface to the first edition of *I Will Not Serve*. It is a curious piece—he warns of the dangers he sees in a "world which has opted for eroticism as opposed to love" and then goes on to give the statistics of suicide in Japan—but what he has to say about Mahyère's death is moving and worth repeating here:

> Concerning this novel, her brother wrote to me: "For me, this book reveals everything that finally drove Eveline to suicide: that mania for the absolute and for the destruction of her loves and of herself." Eveline Mahyère committed suicide on 26 July 1957. She had written a letter addressed to her parents and her brother: "Because you love me, because I love you, forgive me. And above all, forgive my offensive and untrue

reproaches. I implore you, love me enough to tell yourselves that I have never known how to live and that everything is better this way. Love me enough to be happy again. Then perhaps, over there, I shall be, too." A little later she wrote again on a scrap of cardboard that was lying about the kitchen where she'd turned on the gas: "Please thank Madame T. for me and tell her that at last I've managed to smile again (it's true my death amuses me!). It's marvellous to die as if one were doing something entertaining, through the grace of God (let us hope). I love you."

The ambiguous "let us hope" is in English in Eveline's original.

André Bay had not imagined that her depression would "lead to the irrevocable", but it was something Jean Mahyère constantly feared. After her second bout of illness she told him that the best thing she could do would be to kill herself but that she did not have the courage. On the day of her death in Geneva, Eveline's parents were away and she and her brother went to the première of Brassillach's *Bérénice* at Avenches. On their return Jean Mahyère was reluctantly forced to leave her alone in the family flat. She had not wanted to go back to the nursing home where she was convalescing because the matron—the "Madame T" of her suicide note—was off duty. She had once said to her brother: "If I feel desperate enough to do it, I mustn't fail." She did not fail.

I Will Not Serve was published in France a year after Eveline Mahyère's death. Even if they found its subject matter disturbing, her reviewers were in no doubt as to the quality and importance of the novel. Claude Mauriac (*Le Figaro*), recognising the influence of the French moralists, and comparing the writing to Cocteau at his best, proclaimed it "a beautiful and serious" book. In *Réforme*, A. M. Schmidt admired Mahyère's "rigorous obstinacy" in employing words "that are classical, hard, crystalline and precise", and Jean Blanzart, who accorded the novel a full-page solo review in *Le Figaro Litteraire* wrote "the biggest mistake would be to think that what we have here is a banal lesbian affair. It is something far more unusual, far purer and far greater." Eveline Mahyère's novel acquires yet more layers of interest in English, when it becomes a translation of the work of a translator, one who, by the manner of her death classically translated art into life.

Antonia White translated over thirty novels from the French, notably much of Colette and Maupassant's *Une Vie*. This version of *I Will Not Serve* is hers in all essentials. I have altered some ambiguous punctuation, the odd clumsy phrase, and what I feel to be now unacceptably dated expressions and usages. (We have not *telephoned to* anyone in England for a long time.) I found and corrected the occasional inaccuracy—on page two, for example, White had Sylvie "biting" one of the masters, but *gifler* cannot, I think, mean more than "slap". The point, of course, is that no translation is perfect. Getting the mood and tone right are perhaps as important as anything, and

Antonia White is masterly at this. She is also prepared to take risks, to cut sentences in half when English rhythms require it, and where necessary to find equivalents in English for phrases which, if translated precisely, would be nonsense. While it is impossible to be sure that Mahyère would approve Antonia White's translation, it is certain that she would have been sympathetic to the problems, one of which, in this case, proved to be the title. Mahyère's original choice was *Le Sacrilège* with, as a possible sub-title *Vous qui Partagez la Gloire des Anges* (André Bay suggested she call it *Comme Un Délire*). In the end Mahyère decided on *Je Jure de M'Eblouir*—a vow that Sylvie shouts to the sky when she determines to become a painter and to impose her vision on the world. A literal translation of this would be "I swear to dazzle myself", or, if you make the vow implicit "I will dazzle myself", or even "I will blind myself". For "dazzle" the OED gives *confound*; *overpower*; *outshine*; *eclipse*; *strike with surprise or splendour*. Antonia White, in the text, decides on "I swear to astound myself" but rightly, I think, rejected it as a title.

Her solution, *I Will Not Serve*, may not be entirely satisfactory, but its forceful negative is nicely paradoxical, and "serve" sufficiently ambiguous—being at once a rejection of bourgeois standards and a refusal to be obedient to God, the Church and all authority. The title also indicates Sylvie's refusal to serve in the roles that history has sanctioned for women: she will not "stand and wait", but neither will she pursue an active life that conforms to the traditions that men have established. It is a title, too, that reflects Antonia White's adolescent battle against the inflexible authority of the Roman Catholic Church, the subject of her first novel, *Frost in May*, and—albeit less directly—of all her books. Like Sylvie in *I Will Not Serve*, and like Eveline Mahyère herself, Antonia White was expelled from a convent (of the Sacred Heart, at Roehampton). She must have identified strongly with the author of the following:

> Julienne, I know you love God, and the Church, and its organs. Do you really love Sainte-Thérèse—and Mother Marguerite-Marie with her smiling hypocrisy and her obsession with the Rule? You told me one day, with a far-away look in your eyes, that you regarded Sainte-Thérèse as a stepping-stone. Stepping-stone to what?

If the main theme of *I Will Not Serve* is the human need to find God, and thereby a reason for living, it is also a powerful love story, comparable, I believe, to two classic novels of adolescent love, Turgenev's *First Love* and Dorothy Bussy's *Olivia*. There are obvious parallels with the second—but whereas Olivia is increasingly aware of, and feels guilty about, "the mass of physical sensations" that accompany her passion, Sylvie has no guilt about a love which for her is centred not in the body, not even in the heart, but in the soul that, paradoxically, she does not quite dare to believe in: "I love you. (And, contrary to what you suggest, this love is not in the least murky but as bright and blinding as a great fire.)"

Georgina Hammick
Brixton Deverill, 1983

"Gate of heaven, Ark of the covenant," (Sylvie stopped for a moment with her fountain-pen in the air, then went on:) "Virgin most renowned, I am amazed to find myself writing to you. I had no intention of doing so, I had no intention of doing anything. I accepted your decision to be silent, to retire into a fog. Mist veils everything with a soothing charm.

But I am no longer your pupil, you are no longer my teacher. Have you, indeed, ever been? What are you doing at that convent teaching mathematics, you who are all music, harmony, youth? Is it because the nuns allow you to play the organ in their church on Sundays, and in your free time, that you stay there among those old moles?

You are perhaps 25, I am only 17, so you claim the right to put up a wall of respectability between us. But I am an outrage to respectability. No doubt you know that the Mistress of Studies has just ex-pelled me, I must say, very politely. She began by giving me permission to spend a week-end with my parents, and while I was wondering what had earned me this remarkable favour (leave of absence is rare at Sainte-Thérèse) she was writing to my mother telling her that my subversive character and the 'undesirable tone of certain of my letters' made her fear that I might exercise a bad influence on my companions. That, furthermore, I seemed unsuited to the convent regime. And she declared herself ready to give me excellent references if my parents decided to send me to a secular school to finish my studies. Three months before my Baccalaureate! Obviously she must be perfectly well aware that my father, a fierce Calvinist, only delivered me over to Sainte-Thérèse-de-l'Enfant Jésus (as he might have cast me into the lions' den) because I had already been expelled from the Lycée. But, at the Lycée, I at least slapped one of the teachers. At Sainte-Thérèse, all I did was to write to my cousin saying that I loved you. That is what **Mother Marie-Sophie, who delights in rummaging in the boarders' blotters to confiscate clandestine correspondence, calls 'the undesirable tone of certain of my letters'. After all that, she had the tact to leave me to give my parents any explanations that suited me. Naturally I told them that I had spoken ill of the Holy Child and of St. Thérèse. As my father shrugged his shoulders and declared that he would not admit they had any right to expel me for such trifles, I hastily added that I had called God the Pimp of Heaven. I promptly received the slap I didn't deserve, and, since the school year is nearly over, I'm to be given some private lessons and left to work for my 'bac' under my own steam.**

So *that* puts an end to the whole incident and

allows me to go on loving you unbeknown to anyone. Even Mother Marie-Sophie does not know who
you are. In my letter to this cousin who is my confidant, I discreetly called you Éléonore, as I do when
I talk about you to him. I hope you don't hate this
name.

I hope, too, that you don't hate me for writing
to you as I'm doing. In any case, I'd promised myself to tell you that I loved you as soon as I'd left the
convent. But I've got to admit to myself that what
I've just told you is bound to shock you; my imagin-
ary blasphemies will doubtless do so far more than
the reality of the 'crime'. All the same, it's true that
all these good nuns who spend their lives collecting
pennies for him do make God seem a bit like a . . .
But I'm crazy to put myself still more in the wrong.
Julienne, I know you love God, and the church and its
organs. Do you really love St. Thérèse—and Mother
Marguerite-Marie with her smiling hypocrisy and
her obsession with the Rule? You told me one day,
with a far-away look in your eyes, that you regarded
Sainte-Thérèse as a stepping-stone. Stepping-stone to
what?

I'm frightened. I'm frightened of everything
you've never told me, of what you dream about when
you sit at the organ, when you go to your Gregorian
Chant Choral Society, or even simply when you're
getting up in the morning to go off to those classrooms all adorned with revolting little plaster statues

of St. Thérèse. Why did you give up your studies at the Beaux-Arts, when your father is one of the richest industrialists in the North and you were on the point of taking your architect's degree (you see your pupils are well documented) just to come and teach elementary mathematics to daughters of ultra-pious middle-class parents? You will tell me that these girls themselves haven't had time to become ultra-pious yet, but I know very well that it was no delayed vocation for teaching that brought you to Sainte-Thérèse.

There is something that you have never told me, something that I have been able to read in your look when, twenty times in a single lesson, our eyes used to meet over the little plaster statues. It is because of that look that I have left the convent, and the thought of leaving you there behind me is literally intolerable to me. If you do not come to me, I shall carry you off by force with a silken ladder. But you are going to write, aren't you, and say you prefer me to the little plaster St. Thérèses?

I love you.

Sylvie."

Julienne Blessner did not answer this letter.

In the diary she had kept ever since she had known the various shades of meaning of such words as

14

"revolt", "love", "whisky" and "hangover", Sylvie had merely noted:

15th April.

In spite of my contempt for news-items, I must register the fact that I have got myself expelled from Sainte-Thérèse. The event would seem to me quite unimportant had it not resulted in my being expelled at the same time from Julienne Blessner.

16th April.

Luckily, I'm drunk. My mother has allowed me to go to bed after having talked to me about God, my conscience and my sense of duty, but I've carried off the bottle and I'm drinking, drinking, drinking . . .

I am certainly suffering. To drink, to sleep, to die. 'Perchance to dream; ay, there's the rub.'

"Sing, my suffering, sing,
For you are gentler than my mother's voice
Like her, you take advantage of my weakness
But you, my suffering, are unexpected.
Now I am stifling you with little sips
And almost feeling I could sing your praises
For I am drunk, and I delight in drinking.

Young drunkard, hymning wine to drown my
    sorrows
Whereas, in fact, my only drink is whisky.
What signifies a single moment's glory
When the whole world is nothing but tomorrows?
Sing . . ."

17th April.
Nothing.

18th April.
Julienne still does not answer. God? I detest him
now. If he exists, so much the worse for him. Let him
leave me in peace.

19th April.
Please God, make her write to me. I've been mad.
I've jeered at you, I've jeered at her, I'm a monster.
I ask your forgiveness, only do make her write to
me.

On the 20th April, Sylvie flung herself on her
writing-paper.

"Dear Mademoiselle,
If I called you Ark of the Covenant, it was not to
mock the Blessed Virgin but because you are the

16

last link, the last covenant between me and a universe that I respect as much as I revile. Oh, I don't only mean the Celestial City but its colony here below, orders of nuns, parent-teacher associations, solicitors' wives' drawing-rooms, work, family, country, angelic or Gregorian choirs, and—yes, why not?... Protestant sects. After all, Protestantism is where I belong through Papa and Mamma, and I ought to return to it. But I cannot, any more than I can understand, in spite of my admiration for your model, Mother Marie-Sainte-Cécile, what made you choose Sainte-Thérèse-de-l'Enfant Jésus as a refuge. Yes, I know there is a God somewhere. But don't you understand that your silence, for me, is absolute silence, the refusal of God himself to answer?"

Sylvie stopped, wondered for a moment whether her last sentence went too far, blushed violently and folded her letter. Then she had second thoughts and added a postscript: "I shall wait for you at the Racine, rue Racine, between 6 and 7 p.m., Thursday. I implore you, come, or at least answer me. Otherwise I shall wait for you all the days of my life from 6–7 at this same bar."

She slipped the letter in the envelope and went out.

Paris was sinking into twilight. Beyond the roofs and the chimneys a sunset glow still lit up the

17

western sky. In the streets, the lamps seemed as ill-timed as candles prematurely lit round the bed of a sick person who refuses to die. People jostled each other on the pavements, impatient to get back to their own honest lamplight, their dinners and their homes.

For the first time it seemed to Sylvie that she had no home. Her father, a business-man and an uncompromising Protestant addicted to plain living and high thinking, regarded his own life and his family's as a school of virtue. He had subjugated his wife, who saw acceptance of her lot as the only attitude permissible to a Christian matron. But he had given up trying to force his ideas on his daughter whose hostility disconcerted him. He loved her too much not to suffer from it, but not enough to find a way of imposing his authority on her. So, in spite of his principles, he behaved like a weak father. Sylvie never said "at home", as nearly all her schoolmates did, but "at my parents'", and although she resembled them by more than one trait of character —in her own way, she was sectarian—she imagined herself quite alien to them. At Sainte-Thérèse she had felt liberated from her family, a citizen of another world.

With her letter in her hand, she wandered through the dusk. At this hour, her schoolmates at Sainte-Thérèse would be getting ready to stop work, putting books and exercise-books away in their desks before getting up to march off in single file to the chapel. Sylvie lingered on the edge of the pavement while the darkness closed round her. If she passed her Baccalaureate this year, never again would she breathe in that typical, slightly pungent school smell of leather satchels, ink and blotting-paper. Her courage failed her. Now she could only imagine the savour of that school world she had pretended to hate, but that, alone in the twilight of her classroom while the others were in the chapel saying the rosary, she had cherished. At that moment, the chapel, where on Sundays Mother Marie-Sophie insisted on her joining the other girls, was transformed for her into a temple of friendship and love. She had thought she would choke with rage when she had learnt that they prayed for her as a lost sheep, a separated sister, but now the prayers were mute. She was doomed to nothing but solitude and silence, standing there on the edge of the pavement. And this silence, at the hour of the rosary, was rendered almost unbearable to her by the din of the traffic.

She herself had prayed, too. But there was always the image that, for her, embodied all love and all piety, printed on her closed lids as she murmured: "Seat of wisdom, Cause of our joy, Spiritual vessel, Vessel of singular devotion", or, again, "Mystical rose". In her parents' religion, the mother of Christ was only the good, industrious wife of a carpenter, mother of a large family, who had been involved in

19

events beyond her understanding. All things considered, she had always seemed to Sylvie a trifle stupid. So she had never been greatly surprised that, in the end, her son should have said to her: "Woman, what have I to do with thee?"

But, due to the fact that Julienne Blessner considered the Blessèd Virgin the Seat of Wisdom, another figure had imperceptibly substituted itself for the carpenter's wife in Sylvie's now incongruous religion; the woman in the blue cloak who dominated the chapel. In her prayers, this unknown goddess, Mirror of justice, Queen of angels and of patriarchs, had the gentleness and the exquisite, remote courtesy of Julienne Blessner. God, Christ, the apostles and the saints, Jupiter, Osiris, Apollo himself, now appeared to her as so many venerable, sometimes marvellous gods, but her passionate worship was given to Mary, Mother of God. Secretly it included all the goddesses who had peopled all the heavens, with a marked preference for Diana, Joan of Arc and Minerva. Aphrodite frightened her a little. She had presided over too many disasters. Sylvie refused to allow herself to make her the goddess of love.

An enormous lorry had just grazed the edge of the pavement. She glared at it for a moment as if it were "a monster, furious bull, impetuous dragon", then crossed the wide road to go and drop her letter in the box. Perhaps after all it was Aphrodite who had revenged herself by revealing in a dream to Mother Marie-Sophie the whereabouts of the letter with the highly undesirable tone. "*C'est Vénus toute entière à sa proie attachée*", Sylvie raged. They had still been studying *Phèdre* in class the day before she was expelled.

Her letter posted, she was seized with such panic that she had to lean against a tree. If she had been unable to find the right words, adopt the right tone, she had signed her own death-warrant. At seventeen only one expulsion seems fatal: expulsion from love.

Thursday came at last. During the ten years and more that her parents had lived in the Boulevard Montparnasse, there had never been a week when she had not crossed the Luxembourg Gardens, but never yet had they looked to her as they looked that day. It is events that suddenly transform certain places into a stage-setting for our lives. She stared at the trees, the Medici fountain, the statues and the passers-by as if she had never seen them before. They had become the unforgettable scenery and the walkers-on in the drama of one hour, the hour of hope.

However, in the rue Monsieur-le-Prince, she wondered uneasily whether it were not sacrilegious to have suggested Julienne should meet her in a café that, according to her cousin Claude, had a bad reputation. She trembled for fear that her gesture, might seem like a piece of bravado. Then she re-assured herself by thinking that the reputation of the Racine could surely not be known to Mademoiselle Blessner. Had it not been too late to beg Julienne to meet her in the porch of a church, she would have changed the rendezvous. But the neon sign of the Racine shone out on the pavement across the road.

Her throat was dry as she pushed open the door of the bar and plunged into it as if she were going to drown herself. She might empty her father's bottles of whisky, but entering a bar by herself was none the less an undertaking that froze her blood. In the heart of a girl in her 'teens, shyness overcomes all other passions; at that moment she would have parted with her soul to see Julienne Blessner sitting at one of the little tables in the Racine. She felt that everyone was staring at her and customers had, in fact, turned round, surprised at the sight of someone so young.

She made a bee-line for a stool, perched herself on it and shut her eyes. "Whatever happens, I don't give a damn for these people. These women are Gorgons, chimaeras; that man is a satyr; the barmaid is a street-walker. I've come here as I might go to the circus, I shall pay for my drink, I don't have to bother about anyone."

"What will you have?"

She opened her eyes and was dazzled by a face. The blonde barmaid and the chimaeras vanished into thin air, nothing remained but that face, and, above all, the expression on that face. Haughty, aggressively reserved, it was a mask of ice in the vulgarity all about it. The contempt she read in that gaze dissipated the terror inspired by the familiarity of the crowd of customers.

When a quarter of an hour had gone by, she knew that Julienne would not come. At first, the minutes had passed lightly; then heavily; then intolerably. Quarter-past six. Half-past six. Seven o'clock. The minutes no longer belonged to time but to hell.

"Quarter-past seven. I am in the street. There is no Julienne. Julienne does not exist. I can't, and I won't bear it. Still a street and yet another street and there is no Julienne."

The world was crumbling. In her agony, she leant against a wall. A passer-by stared at her, hesitated, then walked on. He turned round several times, intrigued, perhaps moved to pity.

Go away, go away.

What could a passer-by do—come to her aid, take her to hospital? No charitable soul could have understood the absence of Julienne. People pity a man who falls from scaffolding, a woman who loses her husband. Because they suffer? No, only because they have the official right to suffer.

23

26th April.

I cannot endure any more absence. Tears are opaque, indifference suffocating. I would like to die, but how? I am afraid of death. Oh, to be given a stab in the back and die taken unawares!.

29th April.

It's two days now since I touched a school-book. My family is being more and more disagreeable. My father threatens to send me away to look after chickens. I don't give a damn whether he sends me off to muck out farmyards or to preach the gospel. I won't go to my Latin lesson.

Life is breaking down. Mercifully there are moments when I am dazed and can imagine that I am still in the waiting-room. But suddenly I become conscious again of this emptiness inside me, all round me; this scorching absence. I feel myself at the furthest end of time and distance. At the other end, Julienne vacillates and tortures me. All I can do is question empty space and the darkness falling, far away, on the gardens of Sainte-Thérèse. My thoughts lose their way there, get stranded in the streets and those streets wound me; the gardens, the houses, the lamp-posts wound me. Whoever is responsible? Why, in all sleeping Paris, not a life, not a hope and over there, at the far end of the distance, that wound, that boomerang? Sainte-Thérèse is

branded in me with a red-hot iron. Sainte-Thérèse
—or Julienne's bedroom.

30th April.
The good sisters have won. They have hurled me
into the void, uprooted me from life, thrown me to
the wild beasts. Have I got a soul left? I would like
to damn it. Julienne! I would give my most precious
possession; it is nothing to me any more, the desire
for your eyes scorches me so.

For this time, it is not a question of deserving
hell only in imagination.

As Julienne Blessner still displayed no sign of
life, Sylvie adopted the only course that remained to
her: she decided to fall ill. She swallowed three
moth-balls, soaked her feet for two hours in an icy
bath, drenched her head in it then went and lay,
blue-lipped and perished with cold, on her uncovered bed.

Two days later, her mother sent Mademoiselle
Blessner a doctor's certificate stating that her
daughter was suffering from bronchial pneumonia
and had a temperature of 103·6°, along with a cover-
ing letter as embarrassed as it was distressed. She was
afraid Mademoiselle Blessner might take a harsh
view of an action that made her a party to her

daughter's deranged behaviour. But Sylvie refused to do anything to help her own recovery till her mother had sent her former teacher the certificate she had managed to obtain on some pretext from the doctor, when her parents were out of the room. As her daughter's condition grew worse, Madame Ceyvenole had discovered an unsuspected weakness in herself. In spite of her embarrassment, she had complied with what could only seem to her a fantastic whim. She had very nearly asked Mademoiselle Blessner to come and see Sylvie.

After this step, the doctor no longer despaired of bringing down Sylvie's temperature and restoring her to health. Two days later, she at last received the letter for which she had almost consented to die.

"Dear Sylvie,

Your mother tells me that you are ill and that you want to 'certify' me of the fact. Shall I admit that I was beginning to be anxious about you? I have waited in vain for your visit to Sainte-Thérèse. Mother Marie-Sainte-Cécile had told me that she had sent you the School Magazine and that you were invited to the Old Girls' meeting on April 21st. I'd arranged to be free that afternoon in order to see you again but the only person I saw was the fat Madame Jougny (Odette) whom I hardly know: she was only my pupil for three weeks before she got married.

I hope that you will very quickly recover and be a healthy young rebel again. Meanwhile, I'm going to try my best to amuse you for a moment or two of a day that may be slow and monotonous. I wish I were able to have a long chat with you, but unfortunately my days, made up of various kinds of work, are a positive race against the clock. The little time left over from my classes and the innumerable activities at Sainte-Thérèse is eaten up by my choir, my learning the organ and, above all, since term began, by working out the plans for the day-nursery Catholic Action is going to start for children born in prison. I've promised to finish this job in a fortnight from now. To tell the truth, I haven't much idea what amusing thing I can tell you because it's past eleven and, after a day's work, I feel much more asleep than alive. I would rather let my imagination wander and mentally relive our study-course in the Easter holidays and rest a moment under the banana-tree in the cloister of Saint-Bertrand-de-Comminges. We were there together three weeks ago, and I have a terrible craving for that cloister whose calm and solitude I could only enjoy for a fleeting minute between two hordes of noisy, restless tourists. I want its living light, I want the beauty of its capitals, all so different and so graceful (did you look at the last one, on the south side of the arcade of the four evangelists, where a woman is holding two horses by the bridle?), I want its communion with the open air, with the mountains—that concentration of calm and recollection, right in the midst of life. Not withdrawn from the world, but a human, living support for the soul that rises up and bases its flight on it. Heaven is everywhere in that cloister: above the central part, beyond the open arcade that closes in the others, in the splashes of sunlight that brighten the shadows of the covered walks.

But now I am wandering off into the realms of pseudo-literature when I haven't a grain of literary talent. True, it is so late, that perhaps I am half-asleep and dreaming as I write to you. Dear Sylvie, do please tell your mother how grateful I am for her letter and her confidence in me, and be sure that I most certainly don't forget you and send you all good wishes.

J. Blessner."

This letter, which contained not the slightest allusion to the drama through which Sylvie was living, left her, for a moment, abashed and even indignant that her own letters and her torments should not have been taken seriously.

"And, naturally, she thinks she'll impress me by talking about my mother's confidence in her!"

Nevertheless, Julienne was so present to Sylvie in

her "wanderings" that love promptly replaced this brief hatred. But it was a brooding love: she could no longer doubt that she had God for a rival.

"I no longer wish for hell. In any case, isn't it heaven that I love in Julienne? (Unless it's the colour of her eyes.) I owe it to her that, at any rate for a time, she's made me aware of spiritual pre-occupations as something real, whereas up till then I saw them as a meaningless chore, like an imposi-tion. Without her, the Virgin's mantle at Sainte-Thérèse would never have seemed so blue to me. But isn't it insane to devote one's youth to the blue of a mantle? I also owe her the fact of having experi-enced some extremely unpleasant feelings. Because, sometimes, on a Sunday when I watched her pray-ing, I had a sudden conviction that God existed and a very definite impression that my unbelief damned me.

Yet what Julienne experiences in a chapel at the sound of the *Ave Marias* and the *Agnus Dei*, isn't it after all what we—Claude, Albine and I— are looking for when we listen to Charlestons and Blues? Plangency of the *Miserere*, plangency of *Stormy Weather*, what are we asking of Betty Smith or of the monks of Solesmes except the identical longing for death, for infinity, for spiritual fire? And because our *De profundis* is the same, we all experience the same need for communion. They use wine; we, more up-to-date, use whisky.

But Julienne is mad. There's no need for a cloister and a banana tree for all that. Besides, there isn't only the *De profundis*, there's also the *Alleluia*. Certainly life sometimes seems to be terrifyingly futile and absurd, but there are other moments, like this one for example, when I let myself be carried away by a great impetus that drives me beyond the limits of myself. Because, at last, she's written to me, everything appears to me in a different light. The universe is ruled by a mysterious harmony, suffering and sadness are beautiful, just as beautiful as joy. I don't think any mystical fervour surpasses those surges of feeling. Miracles of love, only I prefer a face of flesh and blood to a distant, inconceivable deity. For a few hurriedly scribbled words, for a smile in the turn of a phrase, one would pledge one's life. And life becomes intoxicating. Nothing has really changed, but one looks beyond things. The world is re-created. I feel that a thousand paths are opening up to me.

For the moment, there is only one that interests me, the one that leads to Julienne. What I've got to do is to write her a letter that she can't evade. I thought I was dead in her eyes, her letter has restored me to life. This does not prevent my situation with her from being completely negative. So I have everything to gain and nothing to lose, by taking a risk! But what risk?"

Searching for the spell that would at last deliver Julienne up to her love, she re-read her letter twice, but one does not learn black magic from the *Imitation of Christ*. Impressed by the affection, at once warm and austere, that Mademoiselle Blessner displayed, she was almost about to make honourable amends and write her a letter that was all piety when, at the bottom of the last page, under the signature, she discovered that some syllables had been carefully crossed out. She went over to the lamp, placed the sheet against the bulb, switched on the light and, by scrutinising it hard, deciphered: "See you soon."

These words which, in themselves, would have been enough to overwhelm her with happiness, produced a positive transport of joy. It was no longer a friendly expression or even an invitation, it was an avowal and, what was more, an avowal someone did not dare make.

She pounced on her writing-paper, scribbled "When?", put the sheet in an envelope and sent the maid out to post it by express mail. Then she got back into bed with a temperature of 104° and undertook the task of answering what now seemed to her the tenderest, most eloquent letter it had ever been her luck to receive.

31

"Dear Julienne,

No, I don't remember the woman who holds two horses by the bridle in the arcade of the four evangelists, I only remember the expression of your face when you stopped and stood still in that arcade. Never have I seen so much love and sweetness in your look. I did not know that they were destined for horses. Will you put some on the façade of your day-nursery?

Oh Julienne, I'm not sneering. I know very well that your happy face that day was due to the presence of heaven in those cloisters, to that *concentration of calm and recollection*, but if you found it just in that particular cloister, wasn't it due even more to the beauty of a woman and two horses that I don't remember than to any reflections of heaven? If I had never seen you with that face before, it was because I had never seen you except in a chapel or in classrooms adorned with the art of Saint-Sulpice. At a time when there is so much to build in this world— even churches—even cloisters—are you going to persist in teaching future Madame Jougnys that 2 and 2 are 4 and that $3 + x = 12 - y$?

Sainte-Thérèse is not the ante-room to Saint-Bertrand-des-Comminges. The calm and recollection you dream of are found in the *contemplative* orders. Now, I don't know a woman whose temperament is more active and constructive than yours. Doesn't it

32

seem to you preferable to construct in stone rather than among old maids disguised as nuns?

Fundamentally, I could adapt myself far better than you could to spending my life in that monastery, dreaming and even meditating at the corner of the cloister of the four evangelists. I am not an active creature—you've reproached me for it often enough—and now that I'm away from classrooms and, thanks to my love for you, almost a pariah, I wouldn't mind, if Saint Bertrand hadn't been coward enough to put himself under the protection of the State whose guides slam the door in your face, going and camping under the banana-tree for a while, in spite of the tourists. I should be content just to sleep and nurse my dreams there, whereas you would promptly set about pulling up the weeds. When I was a little girl, and people talked to me about God and the apostles and the wandering monks, I used to dream of going off alone with my deity to sunny lands, with a staff in my hand, and begging my living. It was not that a beggar's life with its poverty and humiliations was attractive to me but it seemcd the acme of freedom and detachment. And I used to repeat to myself, like a sweet song, 'Consider the lilies of the field, they toil not neither do they spin, yet even Solomon in his glory was not arrayed like one of these.'

Even now I still believe that the life of Spanish

gipsies and beggars presupposes more detachment
and disdain than that of French or Spanish bankers.
But we are in Paris and, as I doubt if you will
consent to accompany me to Spain, we shall remain
in Paris. We shall nourish our respective fervours
here, mine for a God who befriends the lilies of the
field, you for a God who uproots the barren fig-tree.
If, as the gospel declares, this God is the same, we
shall meet again. Tomorrow, Julienne, or the day
after. Act quickly. I am still burning with fever but
it is only the fever of anticipation. It is for you to
fix the time and the place.

Desperately yours,
Sylvie."

Because she had put all her heart and soul and
her 104 degrees of fever into this letter, Sylvie felt
that it was a crucial and decisive one. It did, in fact,
make Mademoiselle Blessner write, there and then,
to Mother Marie-Sainte-Cécile, the superior of the
Convent:

"It is with much grief, Reverend Mother, that I
beg you to accept my resignation.

A pupil has been expelled on my account. I do
not think I have committed any sin, either in my
acts or my intentions, but the consequences of this
non-existent sin exist and I feel responsible for them.
I had, no doubt, become too much attached to

Sylvie. I could not continue my work in your house, feeling that I had betrayed what made me undertake it.

We must 'give no offence in anything, that the ministry be not blamed'.

But it is not about myself that I want to write to you. More than any of your pupils, Sylvie Ceyvenole needs your solicitude and affection. Like all her schoolmates, like all the people who have had anything to do with you, she admires you and loves you. I implore you, ask her to come and see you and tell her that she will never see me again.

As I am turning away from her and from this house where I had thought I should build up my life, I beg you to take it on yourself to see that Sylvie works, passes her Baccalaureate, and, above all, becomes a woman animated by the same spirit as yourself.

I entrust her to you and I beg your forgiveness.

J. Blessner."

Mother Marie-Sainte-Cécile to Mademoiselle Blessner:

"My child, I thank you for your trust. I am sorry for you and I pray for you. But take my advice, see Sylvie again and do not abandon us.

Come and see me tomorrow at five o'clock. From now until then, I shall be with you in thought and in all affection.

Mother Marie-Sainte-Cécile."

Mother Marie-Sainte-Cécile did not think that the love of a pupil ought to prevent a mistress from teaching mathematics. The importance Mademoiselle Blessner attached to a mere "professional mishap" seemed to her, quite frankly, cowardly. Moreover, she considered that the best way to conquer sin is to surmount it, not to run away from it.

Her calm and her smile got the better of Julienne's scruples. The young woman sent her former pupil an amiable, impersonal note to invite her to come and hear the Brandenburg Concertos with her at the Salle Gaveau one day in the following week.

11th May.

I don't understand. At Sainte-Thérèse, Julienne often used to stay and talk to me and we exchanged almost conspiratorial smiles. Last night, she behaved like a charitable lady engaged in Good Works. Have the old maids brought her to heel? After the concert, it was only after any amount of demurring that she consented to come and have a soft drink with me.

Sitting over our depressing beverages we hardly knew what to say to each other. That was no doubt why she talked so much, all about the girls at school, the necessity of my passing my Baccalaureate brilliantly, the rain we've had this spring, the various renderings of the pieces we had just heard. I would have liked to talk to her about *her*, about us, but I could not bring myself to utter a word and I listened to her, frozen. However, for one moment, in the middle of the concert, I did see her real face again. I was so violently moved that I dared to take her hand. She did not withdraw it till the sixth bar of the slow movement.

This morning I bought the record of the concerto. Tirelessly, I listen to those six bars and I cry. At the fifth, she gripped my hand in a way people don't ordinarily grip one's hand, as if she were saying good-bye to me before returning to another continent, to her own country. I was unhappy, and yet never has music seemed to me more beautiful. Julienne, do you think that music will remain to me when they have killed you, taken you away from me? Love has multiplied the power of Bach's Fugue in D, of the portrait of Isabella d'Este, of the poems of Henri Michaux, of barrel-organs and street fiddlers. When the architecture of that love has been destroyed, will the architecture of yesterday's concertos produce the same effect on me as it does today?

I want it to. I want you to have given me da Vinci

and Bach for all eternity. Not only your ephemeral presence but their presence that can never be taken away.

13th May.

When she left me, Julienne asked me, in a friendly voice, to telephone her. That was two days ago but I cannot bring myself to do it. Not that I have stopped loving her; I love her ruthlessly, hopelessly, desperately, but if it weren't for the six bars of the slow movement, I should say I meant nothing whatever to her. If she had insulted me, I could have dreamed of fighting and conquering her one day. But she smiled at me as charmingly as possible, almost without seeing me, as if I had been Mother Marguerite-Marie.

I've written to Albine and Claude to do their utmost to meet me tomorrow, Sunday, at the Racine.

In her post, Mother Marie-Sainte-Cécile found a letter from Mademoiselle Blessner. She smiled. "So now I'm promoted to spiritual director," she murmured as she put on her glasses.

"Forgive me, Reverend Mother, if I am being importunate, but I do not feel strong enough on my

38

own to deal with what you call a 'mishap'. It is not Sylvie's sentiments that shock me, but my own. All this evening I have been unable to think of anything but her, though thirty pupils and thirty pieces of homework demanded my attention. Do not urge the parable of the lost sheep as a justification for me; I am not the good shepherd. At most I am a little mathematics teacher who is getting lost in insoluble equations.

You told me yourself—and you were right—that Sainte-Thérèse had given Sylvie all she could expect of it, all that we could give her, and that to take her back into the house again would only unbalance her more than ever. So what can *I* contribute to her good?

My friendship, you would say, and the example of a certain discipline. Up to now, I have only been able to hide my own distress from her by taking refuge, first in silence, then in inhuman politeness. Is *that* a very profitable kind of friendship? Certainly, I hope you will not advise me never to see Sylvie again, but the very fact that I dread this rupture makes me think that perhaps it may be desirable. In the present state of my own feelings, I am afraid I may be unable to be of the slightest use to her. And I am alarmed by the importance she is assuming in my life, which I want to devote entirely to my work and, one day, I hope, to what motivates that work.

With your permission, I am going to try, at any

rate for a time, to devote myself to various tasks that demand all my concentration and all my energy.''

What Julienne Blessner did not admit was that Sylvie seemed to be occupying an excessive place in her life that particular evening because all day she had been waiting in vain for a telephone call from her. Knowing nothing whatever of the reactions of love and vanity, she possibly mistook resentment for the demands of virtue.

While Julienne was asking heaven and Mother Marie-Sainte-Cécile to restore her lost peace of mind, Sylvie, stiffly encased in her despair, remembered that the charms of friendship are less deadly than those of love. Fortified by the resignation that gives even the most impassioned soul the power to make, or not to make, advances, to telephone or not to telephone, she remembered that, since she had drunk her naphthalene love-philtre, she had not seen her best friend, Albine de Cêtres.

Albine belonged to a family that had lost all its money, and Sylvie had always been fascinated by the pleasantly free and easy manners of the Cêtres household. Her own taciturn, vegetarian parents seemed never able to forget that the kingdom of heaven was not of this world. For Madame de Cêtres and her

40

children, that kingdom was replaced by their common youth. Albine's mother had only stopped being a child in order to learn from her own children whose fierce innocence and generosity she shared.

Like many women of her generation, Madame de Cêtres had for a long time paraded her ignorance like an amusing foible, but she had insisted that both her children, the girl as well as the boy, should be sent to the Lycée. Their teachers had never had a better pupil than this mother. As a result of having listened lovingly to her son and daughter recite them, she could have spoken as tenderly of certain pages of Tacitus and Racine as any professor at the Sorbonne.

Monsieur de Cêtres would emerge now and then, like a familiar spirit, from his library where he was completing a mysterious work on the mysterious fauna of the ocean. In spite of the wreck of his fortune, he was incapable of taking his mind off sea-anemones in order to concentrate on cotton-mills or citrus fruits. On Sundays, when he took part in the family life, one might have imagined the household consisted of a dreamy father and three awed children. But he soon retired to his aquaria and his books and then care-free lightheartedness resumed its sway. Yet there was nothing oppressive about his presence. If it was intimidating, it was only because one felt he was locked in his own thoughts from which he was rarely able to distract himself, in spite of his great affection for his wife and children. Now and then he would suddenly rouse himself and enquire with disarming good grace about the small occurrences of family life. At such moments he became the delightful companion he could have been with a little less learning and a less passionate interest in marine biology. But the only link he had with the solid earth was his deep love for his wife. That love was enough to make his home pleasant to his children and welcoming to friends, while Madame de Cêtres' genius was able to expand and hold sway over the household.

This household fascinated Sylvie. To her, it stood for happiness. The austerity of her own parents which, in spite of their natural kindliness, was reflected in the furniture, their way of dressing and the food they ate, seemed to her like a shameful secret vice when she was at the Cêtres'. In their home, she would far rather have been the daughter of a forger or an operatic tenor. She admired Albine's insolence. Indulgent as she was, Madame de Cêtres did not always appreciate the freedom of language and behaviour that her daughter ostentatiously displayed. She had hoped for a time that Sylvie would be an edifying example to her. Soon she had been forced to surrender to the evidence that austerity can produce irreverence as well as prudishness. Perhaps, in her heart, she preferred irreverence.

Although the Racine had been a regular haunt

of Albine's for some time, Sylvie was not certain of
finding her there that Sunday. But Claude, Sylvie's
cousin, would be quite sure to be perched on one of
the stools in the bar. For the past year he had been
pursuing Albine with equal assiduity and lack of
success. Albine admired him, but declared that she
was madly in love with an actor of fifty-five and refused to regard Claude as anything but a confidant.
So many frustrated loves made Albine, Claude and
Sylvie the best friends in the world; they laughed
together over their rebuffs or wept over them in a
'general post' of confidences. Nevertheless, modesty
or fear of ridicule restrained them from bewailing
griefs which, for each of them, was the only grief, so
intense that it bound them to silence. "If I do not
tell my sorrow, it will die with me. Despair already
has its poets and its victims. What could I add to
them? Curious how the grief one experiences oneself
seems appallingly unique."

Nevertheless, it was their capacity for enjoying
themselves that united them, along with their gaiety,
their despair, a common horror of work and the passion to understand. All equally lazy, the three of
them were constantly preoccupied with the art of
doing nothing. They imagined each other rather
than knew each other, and they were bound together
by a kind of sympathetic magic. Sylvie was sometimes amazed at things she said, at certain gestures
she had learnt to make because, mysteriously, these

43

were what *they* expected of her. Ill-mannered, they borrowed each other's rude remarks. Soon each of them was rude enough for three. They had withdrawn from the world into a frail triangular universe on the edge of the void where everything in the way of effort, duty and tiresomeness was suppressed and barred.

How would they have lived had the war and the peace turned out differently? Perhaps that period was their particular period. In another age they might, perhaps, have been exactly the same. But they would have been conscious then of being drifters. In this post-war world they seemed to themselves sages.

Claude reigned over the trio. He had abandoned his family at the age of seventeen and been abandoned by it as soon as he was eighteen. But his grandfather had been delighted to see his grandson escaping from the provinces to Paris, and deserting the chemist's shop where he and his son had drowsed away their entire lives. Presuming that Claude's intention was to realise dreams he had shamefully cherished himself, he had sent him money to complete his literary studies . . . and to play the part of a Don Juan, or rather (the old man was fond of warbling) of a Tino Rossi. But Claude had never consented to further these romantic designs. Thwarted of being a libertine by proxy, and convinced that his grandson was incapable of embracing anything or anyone, the grandfather decided the boy was not worthy to be a prodigal and cut off his supplies. For some years Claude had lived wretchedly in a garret with a skylight in the Rue des Beaux-Arts. At twenty-seven he still obstinately refused to work except when he felt like it, which was seldom. Two years previously, like a rocket bursting in the night sky only to vanish in it, a one-act play of his had been put on at a little theatre and had had a success as dazzling as it was fleeting. But the only thing Claude cared about was the thesis he had set himself to write on the problem of death in contemporary philosophy. He wrote slowly and laboriously, worked little, slept little and was only fully alive in brief, but intense, spasms. For a time he had believed he was a creative genius. Every morning he had scribbled away listening to the radio programme devoted to musical masterpieces. Everything he did, each word he wrote or re-read, seemed dazzling to him against the sonorous background of the overture to *Don Giovanni* or of the *B minor Mass*. Soon he was forced to admit that, more often than not, the elegies he composed were pretty shoddy stuff and he gave up this method of working.

His father had the tact to die. Claude resolved more firmly than ever to devote his life to the refusal of life and of the chemist's shop, but he could now exist with impunity, at any rate until he had run through his inheritance. He rented another attic, with a window and a wash-basin, bought an electric-stove and decided to get up at five every morning in order to write what he had to say concerning the existence of the gods and his own existence. This occupation seemed to him marvellously futile and he felt happy. At night he wandered into the company of the models and whores of the École des Beaux Arts, and nothing struck him as better illustrations of the weighty propositions he had been juggling with all day than the confidences of these tarts. He devoted thirty pages to the metaphysical obsessions of prostitutes.

At rare intervals he dined at his cousin's home or with some bourgeois family. For the whole of that evening he would diligently play the part of the perfect eligible bachelor and make himself adored by the mistress of the house. But Madame Ceyvenole was not taken in.

"Claude has never written except in praise of despair. His poetic enthusiasm saves him from the thing he extols. But Sylvie is at the age when one goes crazy over an idea—in this case contempt and refusal of life—to the point of putting it into practice. I'd rather she'd become infatuated with a cousin who had no brains but was a dentist or a horticulturist."

However, in spite of her love of flowers, it was with Claude and his dizzy paradoxes that Sylvie was infatuated. She was fascinated by this Diogenes who lived in garrets, this sneering angel who, by his refusal of life, placed himself outside life in a falsely Satanic universe. As the hero of revolt, his intelligence and his friendship exercised a spell over Sylvie that justified every kind of negation, whereas Julienne's respect for life and her quiet courage excited her capacities for ardour and hope. Angel of darkness, angel of light. Resolutely, she gave herself up to the sin of angel worship.

That day, she went to the Racine to find the antidote to Sainte-Thérèse—Claude's destructive laugh and Albine's admiring one. She promised herself to fail in her Baccalaureate, to hate life, not to work any more or love any more or eat any more and to drink to the verge of suicide. But life clung inexorably to her seventeen-year-old fibres and she was merely preparing herself to live desperately, not to die.

Die to oneself, the apostles were always harping. She reversed the proposition. "Let everything die to *me*, I want to live by that shambles."

"Claude!"

But Claude was not in a talkative mood. The empty bar, with a friend present in body but absent in mind, was a universe. Luckily, Albine came in and swept her off to a little table while Claude

47

plunged into a manual on criminology. And Sylvie regained the delicious sensation of wasting time instead of being mangled by it, of being aware of Albine and the impact of her crazy equilibrium. Albine enthusiastically admired all Claude's eccentricities and Sylvie's passionate ravings but she was so healthily fond of games, dancing, flirting and whipped cream that no false or noxious theory could have dimmed the brilliance of her cheeks or destroyed her gaiety and her youthful animal zest.

"Tomorrow, I'm going to make love, what d'you say to that?"

". . . . ."

"What d'you think about it? That it's a bad idea?"

"Obviously you've got to do it one of these days. But why tomorrow?"

"Because I've promised your cousin to."

"Promised my . . ."

"Don't shout, he'd be furious if he heard us. I had to talk to you about it; if you think I'm wrong, I won't do it. And I won't do it if it annoys you personally, either."

"My cousin and Albine, they both belong to me in some way and now the two of them . . ." thought Sylvie. She said aloud:

"Perhaps—I don't know for certain—I might have preferred it to be somebody else. Probably because

48

I'd never thought about it. He was the first boy I ever kissed."

"So what d'you think?"

"I think you're right. He kisses very well. And, besides, he loves you."

"*I* don't love *him*. But tomorrow I'm eighteen and I don't want it to be just an ordinary day. It's up to you to decide. I could put it off for a few days and do it with Jacques or Mario Cermati."

"*They* don't love you, either of them. There might at least be a little love in your experiments, Albine."

"I've warned him that I'll give him three minutes, watch in hand."

"You'll have something better to do with your hands."

"With me, he loses all his capacity. There's a clock in his room. At the fourth minute, if he hasn't been able to come up to scratch, I shall get dressed again. I think he's frightened."

He was frightened.

Mario Cermati, who was not in love, was not in the least embarrassed or chilled by the timepiece. Sylvie admired Albine without envying her.

Alone in her room, which, for the past few days, she had only left for the tiresome duty of meals, she lay on her sofa and re-read the letters a man had written her a little while previously; the man whom she had often considered as a possible lover.

12th May.

"My Sylvie,

Since we have decided not to see each other again, there is one thing I can say to you now which is that I loved you almost at once. I have loved very often in my life but always women whom *I* set out to conquer. Today, I can hardly recognise myself. It is definitely because I love something in you other than the physical self that my love renounces the pursuit. Because I love you more than I desire you, I am prepared to renounce you. And yet what a temptation to say to you: 'Sylvie, we're two great idiots.' I know, because I've felt it and because one day you told me what it is you expect of me. Yes, by all means! Let us live! I will teach you. You will belong to me and that will liberate you. We shall come together in the deepest part of ourselves. The future can take care of itself, once our senses are appeased. We will see *afterwards* what is the best thing to do and what remains of our feelings for each other. We shall experience marvellous moments and my caresses will spring from the best part of myself because I love you. Don't let's delay any longer, if we delay we are lost!

I could go on for a long time in this key, one sentence would so easily lead to another and they would bring back all the passion of our embraces.

But I haven't the right to do so, both for your sake and my own. We can expect very much more from one another. You were sixteen when I met you, and it will be some time before we are sure of ourselves. You have your personality to develop and I want you to be able to do so as freely as possible. That is why I have consented not to see you again for months, if that is what you want. All the same, one day, you will have to judge and to make up your mind; you will have to learn to know me and my past and to find out if it is possible for us to love one another. I could almost be your father and, in any case, a man always has a past. *You* are too young for that. All the same, perhaps, when you answer my letter, you could tell me whether it is the friend or the lover you want. Or whether, after all, it is neither, which would explain your violent changes of mood about me. Tell me, with your innocent cynicism, to whom do you address yourself in me? The mistress to her lover, or the friend to the man who will one day perhaps be her husband . . . or a passer-by?

> Your
> François."

14th May.

"I am too frightened of your answering my last letter not to write this other one at once. I gave you the choice between the husband and the lover as a more or less long-term policy. Because I was afraid of myself, afraid of degrading you, I agreed not to see you again for the time being. But I have not told you enough about what, in spite of all my desire for you, I hope from you. All my life, I have longed to find my own counterpart in a woman, and I believe—in my dreams—that you are that woman. That is why I want you to become *my* woman, my wife, that is why I am ready to wait a long time for you. No, I do not want to make you my mistress.

But perhaps you are just simply a young girl who, at sixteen, found me attractive as a novelty, as her first encounter with love and virility. As time went on, you realised that your unknown stranger was a human being much like any other man. And you are continuing your life of a little girl avid for knowledge and discovery.

I cannot rule out another possibility—that you have met another man and that, according to the fervour of your feelings for him, according to whether you feel satisfied or disappointed, I fade out or you come back to me a little.

Don't play with me any more, Sylvie, tell me how things stand. There are so many paths in life. Couldn't we follow the same one?

François."

Sylvie dropped the two letters on the floor and began to scribble in her diary.

17th May.

He agrees not to see me any more for weeks, for months, and now I've got to reply to a proposal of marriage! To a chemist!

Claude, Julienne, it's you two I love. With you, Claude, things appear as they are: a baited trap. Even love—love most of all. With you, Julienne, things and that trap don't exist because you live in a kingdom that is not of this world.

But *I* can't conceive the world without you. Sleeping with François or with Claude, doing Latin proses, taking a degree in philosophy? Doping myself ad nauseam with other people's certainties, their more-or-less accepted false ideas. What else? Eternally asking myself whether all this is more or less true, whether it isn't a dream that will have no awakening, or rather, whose awakening will be death . . .

So why not die at once? But death definitely frightens me. If one wants to live and to retire from the world, one has to choose between three houses where one is shut up; the asylum, the convent and the brothel. I'm wearing myself out dreaming too much of all three of them. Julienne! I asked you for the key of life. If you gave it to me, would I know how to use it? I abandon the case of my life and my death to the specialists. Without you, despair becomes tedious and hope exhausts me. I delighted in mixing my brain with my heart but I was never able to blend them. Dangerous cocktail; my feelings have falsified my intelligence but without making me blind. But any coherence would inevitably destroy me.

Here I am at the end of my frenzy; night fades without a dawn; after alcohol comes the void. Through these sleepless nights and these paroxysms, shall I discover the final answer? Too cowardly to find it, I live by seeking it.

Telephone Julienne! Write to Julienne! And not marry that chemist. . . .

Like a drowning man clutching at a buoy, Sylvie grabbed her writing-paper.

17th May.
"Architect of dreams, distant Éléonore (oh, I know you're called Julienne) how can I make you understand, without poetical exaggeration, what the minutes of this unbearable time are to me? If it were to last another twenty-four hours, I should explode into madness. Luckily, one gets exhausted. But the nights return. After having made me experience the bright shock of day, are you going to send me back to their barbarous delirium? I won't telephone you. I cannot stand destroying myself any more by encountering the icy personage you have

54

chosen to confront me with. When you're alone, you remove this mask; by writing to you I may hope it is really you who are reading my letter.

Mademoiselle Blessner, we are faced with an irrevocable fact: we know each other. There is no going back on that. I mean that it is too late to demand the least indifference from me. I know that your silence is an escape, I don't want any more juggling with truths. To see you again, have I got to act and pretend and calculate? What an awful undertaking! If you insist, I'll set myself to the job. But I owe you the cruel consideration of a warning. (Haven't you been, up to now, my only attempt at absolute honesty?) You will learn—at my expense—that frenzy is not at all to your taste. Do not confuse it with violence, its ruler. Mad people are not the heroes whose parts they seem to assume. I would like to spare you their tiresome manias, their absurd reflexes. I would like to spare myself their periods of convalescence, they are too deadly. It's hard to recover from one's shattered dreams.

But your face is not a face of dreams and catastrophes. You look like those angels who bring good tidings, and I will banish the thought of mirages and their vanishing act.

Answer me. That's all I want, nothing more. If our meeting is to be a good thing, not an evil one, you must help me.

Sylvie."

18th May.

"Sylvie, I do not know how to answer you. You express in words, in phrases, things that perhaps do not exist and that embarrass me like delirious ravings. My own life is very simple: I do my job as well as I can, I make an effort to live as uprightly as I can. I had become greatly attached to you, it is true, but I saw nothing murky in my affection for you. Why have you had to distort everything so that now I am frightened of thinking of you and yet never stop thinking of you?

I want to see you. But I have very little free time. How can we meet? Would Wednesday evening at 9 suit you? Tell me where to meet you.

Yours sincerely,
J. Blessner."

18th May.

"Dear Julienne,

I don't want to meet you in a bar, still less in the parlour of Sainte-Thérèse; it would seem like going to visit you in my former prison. On the other hand, all public places seem to me like railway-stations, I should hate to meet you in a waiting-room. My cousin has a room he is not living in at the moment*:

---

* The attempt at absolute honesty adapted itself quite happily to this lie. The most serious disadvantage of this slight "sin" was that it put Claude under the necessity of committing a graver one by spending the night elsewhere.

56

5 Rue des Beaux-Arts, under the roof, at the end of the passage. You get to it by the staircase on the left of the courtyard. I'll be waiting for you there on Wednesday at 9.

As I'm too frightened that you'll write or telephone to say that a tête-à-tête in an attic bedroom shocks your principles, I'm just about to take a train to the country where I shall spend two days with an aunt 'preparing a French essay'. I shan't return till Wednesday evening so that, come what may, I shall be waiting for you.

I love you. (And, contrary to what you suggest, this love is not in the least murky but as bright and blinding as a great fire.)

Sylvie."

20th May.

This meeting, I had longed for it so, hoped for it so, that I didn't dare believe in it. At five-past nine I was convinced that Julienne would not come. I wandered from the divan to the chest-of-drawers, from the window to the door, incapable of sitting down and waiting. I no longer knew where I was or what I was doing, the minutes slipped by without my knowing it. When, at 9.30, someone knocked at the door, I opened the door, completely taken aback. Julienne materialised in the dimness, an almost colourless shape. She was wearing a tailor-made suit of some neutral colour and wore not a single piece of jewellery and no make-up. But her fair hair threw a brightness round her face. She seemed very embarrassed. I was even more so. I had imagined this moment as one of the happiest of my life and now all it was bringing me was a sense of discomfort.

'—I ... I'd given up hope of your coming.'

She sat down in the only armchair, without replying. At last she murmured: 'I'm late, forgive me. I wavered between Saint-Germain des Prés and the Rue des Beaux-Arts for exactly half-an-hour.'

'Are you frightened of me, then?'

'I don't know.' Obviously she did not want to dwell on this delay. 'You very nearly put me off coming by your extravagant behaviour. But I particularly wanted to see you.'

There was so much tenderness in her voice that at last I felt joy flood over me. It was as if the light and the darkness had begun to shine all round me, inside me. For the first time since my expulsion from Sainte-Thérèse, Julienne had really wanted to meet me again. Yet something in her still paralysed me, her extreme reserve, her shyness perhaps; I wanted to throw myself at her feet, cover her with kisses, but I dared not move.

Precipitately, she stood up, and said, with a kind of violence: 'I want to talk to you about friendship.'

She paced up and down the room and seemed only half conscious of what she was saying. I was not listening. I took in the intonations and the tone of that voice as if it were the oxygen I was breathing. I was living on it. I understood each one of the words and the meaning of those words but what they signified mattered little. The intonation told me as much as I needed to understand.

She spoke to me of friendship as a privileged encounter between two people, as a feeling made up not only of tenderness but of mutual esteem. And suddenly, as if she had grasped how utterly little I care about succeeding or not in the Baccalaureate, she halted in front of me and said almost earnestly:

'If you love me (she said "If you love me" and not "If you are my friend"), you will pull yourself together and make the effort to work and to pass your exams. I wouldn't have any respect for a person who gives up.'

'If I'm giving up, it's because I don't want to tire myself out for an academic formality that means nothing whatever to me.'

'And what does mean anything to you?'

'You.'

She looked at me angrily, as if I had used an indecent word. Yet I had not said it out of defiance. Only she and what she embodies for me have any importance in my life. I am sure that, for Patroclus, the war was only a solid reality because he was fighting it with Achilles, for Achilles. But what war can I embark on with Éléonore? Definitely not real war,

59

for I loathe sport and if, one day, women were mobilised like men, soldiering, even with Julienne, would undoubtedly revolt me. Yet what voluptuous joy to die at her side!

She must have realised that her remarks about the virtue and necessity of the Baccalaureate had fallen on deaf ears, because she resorted to sentiment.

'Prove to me that you care for me, by working.'

'And by having a lot of children?'

She seemed disconcerted, then she began to laugh. She realised that I had simply announced the programme that Sainte-Thérèse set out for all its 'daughters': Baccalaureate, marriage, motherhood. I was seized with a fit of rage.

'I'll give you a different proof that I care for you. You're twenty-five, you're an architect or very nearly one. In a few months, you could return to what used to be your life and live. I've nothing to offer you, yet I have the feeling that it's your life and my life that I've got to rescue from a spell: You've chosen slow death. Don't deny it. You wouldn't be here if I were lying.'

I hated her. I adored her. I was worn out with beating my head for so long against a wall, from imagining her a prisoner in that convent that had rejected me. I knew from a friend of Claude's who had worked in the same studio with her at the Beaux-Arts how much her plans had been admired and how much everyone had been impressed by her personality. But she had been fated to come in contact with Mother Marie-Sainte-Cécile and the dove of the Holy Ghost! It's all incomprehensible to me. Yet I know Mother Marie-Sainte-Cécile and I cannot help liking her. Once, I even believed that some day she would convert me. But as soon as I realised that Julienne had completely abdicated to her, I dug my heels in. It is not God that I hate. It is the use His faithful make of Him. I admire Mother Marie-Sainte-Cécile but I don't want the other nuns at Sainte-Thérèse for 'Sisters in God' at any price.

I must have looked like an animal who had contracted rabies. Julienne stared at me, petrified. I took fright. Wasn't I going to drive her away from me for ever? A sudden inspiration saved me from disaster.

'If you promise me to come back in a week's time, I'll work during that week.'

She did not tell me that it was blackmail. She knows too well, from having so often reproached me for it at Sainte-Thérèse, that, as long as I am not sure what I want to do in this world, as long as I have not found a decisive reason for living, I shall do nothing. Or anything I do, I shall do only for her. I have no intention of working in order to become a bluestocking, or the mother of a family, or to buy myself a sewing-machine. Rather than live just for the sake

61

of living, I would prefer to spend my time watching flies. But one day I shall know what I live for, and then, if necessary, I'll drudge and toil, I'll kill myself at the task.

For the moment only one thing matters to me—Éléonore. I want her to come back and she has promised to come back. So I am going to abandon my diary and work till I'm dropping with sleep.

Sylvie's resolution was thus a mixture of friendship, love and childishness. Mademoiselle Blessner, who was not yet entirely anaesthetised by her religious fervour, was half embarrassed, half delighted by it. On returning home, that evening, she once again felt the urge to write to Mother Marie-Sainte-Cécile. There are people in whom, even when we see them every day, we only dare confide on paper.

"Dear Reverend Mother,
I have obeyed you. I am seeing Sylvie again. And I think that, at last, my friendship is being of some use to her because she has promised me to work, whereas, ever since she was expelled, she has obstinately refused to do so. But shall I confess to you that it was cruelly hard for me to urge this child to live normally when I myself am preparing to abandon for ever what for so long I believed to be life?

I remember my happiness and excitement the day I passed my entrance examination to the Beaux Arts. I felt as if I were going to rebuild the world. I know now that man is not lord of creation but that he must be constantly subject to his Creator. I felt myself 'called to you'. That is why I came to work with you.

But I am beginning to doubt myself and what I believed I could call my vocation. Am I really made to live and work and pray at your side? When I hear Sylvie reproaching me for having given up my architectural studies, I miss architecture. Is it my profession, or the image Sylvie has made of it in her own mind and presented to me, that confuses my feelings like this? I think of you, of that extraordinary clarity you brought into my life the day you said to me: 'Come, my child. We are made to work together in God's service.' And I suffer, because I feel unworthy of your trust. Tonight, my only hope lies in your affection.

Julienne."

"My little Julienne,

I am thinking of you very specially at this moment and I am going to tell you so, though my fingers are quite stiff with rheumatism.

I want my thought to penetrate into yours to bring you light and strength, and my affection to go

63

deep enough into your heart to revive it with courage and hope.

Tell yourself firmly that our souls are subject to doubt and weakness and that only prayer permits us to triumph over our uncertainties. I am praying for you. All the community is praying for you. Isn't that a rampart that you must feel protecting you? Have trust in God. Whether your destiny is to be an architect or to remain among us, if you submit yourself to His will, your life will be inundated with light. We must never lose contact with each other. I am always at your disposal. And I embrace you with all my deep affection.

Mother Marie-Sainte-Cécile."

As she read this letter, Julienne experienced the joy of a blind man who has recovered his sight. She no longer doubted that, for her, happiness lay in a total renunciation of what Sylvie pompously called life, and Mother Marie-Sainte-Cécile's affection did indeed seem to her a rampart against all the uncertainties Sylvie had aroused in her. But she felt obscurely that, in struggling against Sylvie's fantasies and rages, she was having to struggle just as much against what remained of her own youth. And this feeling—it was not a thought, for one never formulates such things to oneself—embittered her joy.

Nevertheless, day after day, Sylvie worked, with

uncharacteristic intensity, till far into the night. Her parents, astounded, became almost uneasy. But never had she appeared in better health, never had she seemed gayer and more amiable. Monsieur Ceyvenole saw in this a confirmation of the opinions he had always held about the joys of hard work and accomplished duty.

Claude had not returned to Paris. Sylvie, who had the keys of his room, often went and took refuge there when she found the atmosphere of family life too stifling. She was surprised at Claude's absence, but, carried away by the wild excitement of Julienne's approaching visit, it did not occur to her to be alarmed by it. Her cousin had often disappeared for a few days.

Julienne's second visit destroyed her fine scaffolding of illusion and hope. Mademoiselle Blessner appeared only to have come in order to keep her word. Sylvie offered her *petits fours* with a secret desire to cry; she was incapable of finding words that would tear off that mask of absence she knew only too well. When, after an hour, Julienne went away, alleging that she had a tremendous amount of work to do, Sylvie did not dare ask her when she would come again. She lived through two days of bleak despair.

A letter from Claude informed her that he had resolved not to return to Paris and to retire for a time to his province to work. Sylvie read this letter as if it might contain the key to all desertions and all despairs.

"You can use my room as much as you like. I don't want to reappear until my friendship for Albine has triumphed over this absurd and laughable sentiment that, from my point of view, love is. If I did not love her, I might perhaps recover some friendly feelings for the person in question. I should no longer see her as anything more than the attractive animal you know, and that I used to know, and I should rediscover all the healthy animal in myself. I've had enough of turning myself into a sentimental shop-girl. Nothing like the charming farmers' wives I meet in the neighbourhood of the country house where I'm living at the moment with my mother, for boosting my virility. And yet—I can admit it to you—I miss Albine and my fine sentiments. I miss that intense illusion of living she gave me. But I have resolved to work, and I don't want to go on any longer with this unspeakable waste of time that love is, even when the love is not shared.

I'm not finding it easy to write. The poet in me is dead. For a long time I could write about the world I used to mingle with my daydreams when I was a child. But, today, the magic of cemeteries, of the yews nourished by the dead of my family, of the

66

golden light of spring on the tombs, seems to elude me. The song of the fountains surrounded by watering-cans is silent. Yet that was the first garden of my childhood, every Sunday, before tea-time. Grandfather Bordier, Aunt Catherine and all the uncles I had never known, peopled my reveries. Already I imagined them mocking at the living who were so slow to understand that they were only the potential dead, that they could be dead any time they liked instead of whirling round and round like distracted mayflies. I thought of death as a friend. When I grew up, only life seemed to me inexplicable. I desire death but I want to be possessed by death, not to rape it. Suicide remains a gesture of the living. As I grew older, I tried to understand why I stubbornly persisted in remaining alive. I read hundreds of books, I revered innumerable men, professors or glorious illiterates. And I realised that it is just as futile to question the living about life as the dead about death.

I have returned to this countryside which I thought I hated because I lived here among people whose flabby imbecility I did hate. Moreover, I rather despised myself for hating. Both my furious dislikes and my enthusiasms seemed to me equally ineluctable, part of the game of life, but contemptible. I have rediscovered a countryside drenched in golden light, the charm of its greenery, the dense sunshine on the sward, the light song of the starlings. And I have been unable to stop myself from loving it. To-night, in the bus, I felt all the old sense of marvel that night used to induce in me when I was a school-boy. That excitement of being in a vehicle, at night. Street lamps threw out soft fingers of light on the pavement, on an old wall, on familiar, sleeping houses. The world was revealed only in glimpses; now a square would appear and vanish, now a branch would tremble. The night spread over the little town like a lake, dammed here and there by lamp-posts, by electric shop-signs and illuminated hoardings. We were sailing along beneath this lake and the blue stretches of night hung over our vaga-bond ship. The earth, the entire earth was nothing but an island, immersed in shadows, peopled with lights. But, in the morning, when I woke up in my mother's house, my sense of exaltation had gone. I was conscious again of the heaviness that seems to flatten out provincial life, that little world where there are no exhibitionists, no dandies, no thorough-bred dogs, where you are expected to live as if the horizon were a wall. I wandered about the streets where I once raged with the fever of adolescence. Neither the roofs, nor the façades, nor even the trees have changed, but the people I met stared at me, hesitating whether to greet me, embarrassed by hav-ing grown older or by my having grown older. Most of the girls I had made love to had become geese occupied in fattening up their goslings. They looked

68

so overblown that I hastily returned home. I no longer want to bother about anything but random affairs with farmers' wives, and the rather melancholy book I am writing.

Tell me about yourself and Éléonore and Albine. You represent all the tenderest, youngest, most feminine part of myself. I shall see you again soon.

Claude."

In spite of Claude's absence, Albine's and Sylvie's friendship lost none of that complicity in rebellion that gave it its savour. Every time Sylvie met Albine she felt the impact of a force, of all the forces with which a violent and unscrupulous person under twenty overflows. Albine was burning with unused energy that made her bitterly regret all the careers that were denied her—aviator, Foreign Legionary, explorer.

"When I think that that feeble object, my brother, thinks about nothing but playing tennis and running after girls, that his sole ambition is to be a solicitor or a stockbroker while I—I can only be stuck here and go round and round in circles, when if I were in his place . . ."

"But nothing forces you to stay here . . ."

Sylvie spoke earnestly, feeling like a mentor. She did not dislike acting the part of bold, wise, mature counsellor to a friend of her own age, even though that friend had infinitely more good sense and zest for life than she had herself. She owed her reputation as a precocious and intelligent girl to the fact that she was the living symbol of rebellion and contempt for rational solutions. This was why Albine was fond of her.

"I'd give my most precious possession for my uncle to die. He's a disgusting, mean old man. But he owns an aeroplane and he hasn't any children."

"Don't go and imagine that a disgusting, childless uncle has only got to die for you to acquire an aeroplane and fly round the world. I should think you've got lots of relations. Seems to me there are other ways of travelling."

"It isn't travel I want. It's to rape the world, to discover it freely, dangerously, like . . . oh, I don't know . . . Alain Gerbault, Lindbergh."

"Why don't you go and see Ginette Collard? She's giving a series of lectures on Tibet and the Indies. She's been there, she's done the very things you daydream about."

"I'm not daydreaming."

"Now you're getting rabid."

"Well, she had the luck to be able to go. It was all due to circumstances."

"Also to her own will, presumably."

"And what would I say to her? She'd laugh in my face."

"If you know how to approach her, no."

"I wouldn't know. Come with me."

Sylvie was seized with a kind of vertigo. For a moment, she was overwhelmed by the temptation to substitute herself for Albine, to adopt her tastes and her fervent enthusiasm, to steal her dream. She would go by herself to Ginette Collard and would say point-blank: "I want to go with you."

But one cannot assume a borrowed destiny. Curiosity and friendship got the better of her; she promised to accompany Albine.

There were a great many people at the lecture Ginette Collard was giving on one of her earlier expeditions to Nepal. Looking at the photographs the explorer displayed on the screen as she talked, Sylvie was overcome by an irresistible desire to doze off. Amateur photos, whether of Nepal, Arizona or the valley of Chevreuse struck her as ineffably boring to anyone who had not seen the places themselves. She only woke up when the lights were switched on again in the hall. Now it was a matter of acting quickly. Already, society females and a journalist armed with a flash-bulb were surrounding the explorer. Sylvie grabbed Albine by the arm and rushed forward, her head lowered, as if she were about to charge the enemy.

"I'd like . . . I'd like to interview you."

"For which paper?"

Ginette Collard had replied in a cool, amiable voice.

"I don't know . . . Actually, it's a paper that doesn't exist. At least, not yet. But I've promised to do a long article on you for the first number."

"Come and see me on Monday at five o'clock."

Albine had not uttered one word.

"Why ever did you lie like that?" she burst out as they were leaving the hall.

"Because she wouldn't have invited us to come and have tea if I'd asked her straight out."

"And what are you going to say to her?"

"She'll do the talking. After that, you will."

"It's sheer fraud."

"Precisely."

Sylvie felt resentful. Albine's reproach seemed to her ungrateful. Yet she had to admit that she herself had a direct interest in this sham interview. Albine's taste for adventure could only be a passing whim, but what were they like, these women who go off to conquer difficult places for no other reason than to pursue the horizon? Ginette Collard had often refused to join organised expeditions, so as to experience her own adventure in solitude. She was the type of woman who lives entirely in terms of herself, independent of a man, a family or a community. Sylvie had high hopes that she would find her a glorious revelation of insolence and pride.

In spite of their admiration for audacious women, both she and Albine felt extremely timid as they rang the explorer's door-bell at five o'clock the following Monday. To their astonishment, a boy of about fifteen opened the door to them and promptly announced that he would go and fetch his mother. They could never have imagined that Ginette Collard would have taken the trouble to produce children between her expeditions. They were surprised by the warm, unreserved welcome they received. Ginette Collard seemed to have guessed their trickery and been amused by it.

"What is it you wish to hear my views on? I don't imagine you want me to tell you the story of my life; I've done that at length in five or six books. But perhaps you haven't had the courage to read them?"

Sylvie blushed violently. She had only read one of them. Albine, who was completely ignorant even of their titles, preserved her composure. This was no longer an interview but an adventure, and she had recovered all her boldness. She felt it was up to Sylvie to do the talking.

Sylvie decided not to beat about the bush.

"I want you to take my friend with you next time you set off."

Ginette Collard raised her eyebrows, then burst out laughing.

"Have you a lot of money, then? Do you know

73

how much a passage from Marseilles to Bombay costs?"

Albine lowered her head, discomfited.

But, because she was not personally involved, Sylvie did not let herself be overawed.

"No, but surely it's possible for a person to raise money."

Ginette Collard studied Albine for a moment. The girl had an enchanting, obstinate face that repaid her attention.

"If you can raise a big enough sum, and if you're capable of driving an old Ford over very rough tracks, there's nothing to prevent you from setting off at random. But who's to tell me whether you've really got the taste for adventure?"

"I do," declared Sylvie.

"And so do I," said Albine calmly. "What you're doing is exactly what I want to try. To go off, I'd be prepared to take a job as a washer-up on a boat, if the chance turned up."

"That kind of chance doesn't *turn up*, you have to go and look for it in a port. But I like you and I'd like to be able to help you. I think I was much the same as you are at your age. Only I had the luck to have an ethnographer for a father, which made it easier for me to undertake my first expeditions."

"The awful truth is that I haven't any money," Albine confessed piteously.

74

"You've an uncle who's got some and doesn't use it. It's a question of making him cough up."

"Whether he 'coughs up' or doesn't cough up," the explorer said gaily, "why do you come to *me*?"

"Because I'm under age and my family wouldn't allow me to go off alone. That's the only reason why I came to see you," replied Albine without bothering about how rude such an admission might sound.

"*I* have other reasons," Sylvie hastened to say, feeling slightly embarrassed. "I wouldn't follow your example for anything in the world, life in the raw doesn't appeal to me. But I admire you. For me, you represent a kind of archetype. That's why I thought of you when Albine told me she wanted to rape the world."

"It's not a question of rape, but of discovery. Believe me, you have to approach the world with a great deal of humility if you want it to bring you what you set out for."

"After so many journeys, aren't you tempted to remain in Paris?" Sylvie asked insidiously. "Ella Maillart wrote somewhere: 'What is the purpose of sending people all over the world? I know, from experience, that ranging the world serves no purpose but to kill time. One returns just as unsatisfied as one set off.' "

"Ella Maillart is a mystic, that is why, for her, travelling was only a pretext, an escape. She went

75

off to ask the sages of India for what she could have found at home, in her own armchair, by reading St. John of the Cross or St. Teresa of Avila."

"Yet she's written books that excite the passion for travel."

"Actually, I think that, in her, it was a passion that drove her to want to exceed the bounds of possibility. For me, and for women like Gabrielle Bertrand or Alexandra David-Neel, exploring Asia was something quite different. The straightforward, simple joy of physical effort, risk and intense curiosity. I discovered the Indies and, little by little, they became a homeland to me, my own province without the pettiness of a province. After a few months of Parisian life, I have only one desire—to go back there and live the life I like, reading and writing. And also to find myself back among people who don't paralyse me, where there are no such things as concierges or society ladies or income-tax officials. People who can't read or write, for whom an aeroplane is quite simply a bird that makes a lot more noise than the others and has a man inside it."

"Hasn't the fact that you're a woman been a handicap in leading the life you've led?"

"I never was, and never shall be, a woman like other women. Perhaps that's why your question loses its point. But do you suppose that men explorers are like the office workers or business men you see in the Metro? You'll tell me that most adventurers have

been men. I quite agree. But when I'm alone in the
desert or the bush, my solitude loses nothing of its
force and grandeur, just because, when I come back
to urban life, I wear skirts."

Sylvie exulted. She could not have experienced
more intense satisfaction had she been given this
answer by Joan of Arc or the Queen of the Amazons.
As for Albine, she felt that, for the first time, she
had met a woman whom she wanted to equal. She
kept silent, but Ginette Collard seemed to be more
impressed by the resolution and defiance she read in
her look than by anything Sylvie could say.

It was agreed that as soon as Albine had managed
to raise enough money, she could come and see the
explorer again.

"I don't commit myself to anything," Ginette
Collard told her. "But I'll see what I can do to help
you. Only don't forget that I reckon to leave Paris
five months from now."

When they found themselves once more in the
street, Sylvie exclaimed:

"You've absolutely got to get your uncle to make
up his mind to lend you this money. *I'll* write the
letter. You know how to act but you've no idea how
to compose a tactful letter."

"All I need is enough money for the outward
journey. For the return one, I can always get myself
repatriated. The tiresome thing is that I'll have to
get my family's consent."

"Your parents aren't the sort who get in a nervous flap about everything. I'm sure you could manage to talk them round."

It almost seemed to Sylvie that this enterprise was her enterprise. She possessed, in the highest degree, the gift of identifying herself with her friends. She wrote a letter for Albine, taking great pains to make it all archness and charm, and got her to send it off at once to her uncle. She was sure that this old man, who was loathed by his entire family, had never received such a pleasant one. True, it contained a request for money, but Sylvie had formulated with it a deliberate ingenuousness that she hoped would be disarming.

She left Albine in a state of high excitement. But when she found herself back in Claude's room, she experienced a feeling of solitude that bore no resemblance to anything Ginette Collard might experience in Asia. She was suddenly conscious of feeling that all the people about her had discovered the true object of their existence, whereas she was content to play with her life while, far away, Éléonore was escaping towards the stars.

Out of weakness, and also because she liked him, Sylvie telephoned François. But she felt nothing in common between herself and this chemist who spent the greater part of his time working in his laboratory for the sole purpose of making money. True, he had a certain contempt for morality and established convention, which was doubtless why Sylvie's subversive character had attracted him.

He came to fetch her, looking radiant.

"It was a good hunch of yours to telephone me today. We're going to have a wild evening. I've just made a million francs."

"By doing what?"

"By transforming gold ingots into coal for a black prince who wanted to get them across the frontier."

"*What?*"

"You forget that I'm an excellent chemist."

Sylvie began to laugh.

"And a smuggler?"

"I'm not the one who's getting them across."

He had thrust the million francs he had just been given into the outer pocket of his jacket, which was thus swollen to bursting-point, and simply fastened it with a safety-pin. This casualness delighted Sylvie.

He took her to a restaurant that was like a winter garden, it was so full of flowers and green plants. Each table was set in a kind of arbour. The mixture of aperitifs, wines and spirits made Sylvie's heart glow with a warmth that soon made her love everything about her. She felt as if she had swallowed some magic elixir.

"We're going to drink, aren't we?" she said, her eyes shining. "Drink till . . ."

"Why are you so fond of drinking?"

"Till at last we're happy."

Two tables away, a woman of forty was leaning over towards a boy hardly older than Sylvie and weeping into her plate. Her unhappiness was a torture to Sylvie. She had never seen a woman of that age crying.

"François, why is she crying? Why?"

"Because that boy, who could be her son, has just told her he doesn't love her."

"How do you know?"

"It's obvious."

Indeed, it needed no more than a quick glance at the young man's cruel, triumphant face and the woman's defeated, imploring expression to prove him right. It was only a scene such as one might see in any restaurant, but it was the first time Sylvie had seen a grown-up person go to pieces. It gave her a shock. She had never imagined that, at forty, one could still sob.

"Let's leave this place. Take me somewhere where there's nobody crying."

He took her on a tour of the night-clubs. For him they represented a perfectly conventional background, so he was amazed at Sylvie's surprise and repugnance at the spectacle of the various crooners, ballerinas and strip-tease artists who performed for

80

their benefit. They wandered from club to club, getting more and more drunk.

Finally, they ended up in the bar of the Racine. Lately, Sylvie had come to know almost everyone there, the students, the shop-girls, a man who had once been in the Foreign Legion. She liked the records they played there, she liked these boys and girls and their friendship, a friendship as fleeting as the mist on the panes, so frail yet so intense.

With his hand on his heart, the ex-Legionary declared:

"I was born in Budapest, a youthful error."

A woman who served in a chemist's shop came up and clinked glasses with Sylvie, sighing: "I drink to forget that I'm drinking."

They were all alike. They were chasing a dream and buying it at the cost of hiccups and liver attacks.

Suddenly, François appeared to remember that Sylvie was only half his age. In a thick voice, he declared, as if suddenly overwhelmed by his responsibility: "I forbid you to drink any more."

"I shall be ill, I know I shall. But meanwhile I'm making life absolutely dazzling. Everything's marvellous in the light that shines up from my glass, you, me, the street-lamps, paradise. Be an angel, take me away and show me other miracles."

"You're too far gone to know what you're saying."

"Take me home with you. I love you."

"If I were a swine, I'd pretend I believed you."

"Be a swine . . ."

He did not hesitate to comply.

When they found themselves in each other's arms on his divan and had turned off all the lights, the darkness began to dance round them.

"What do you see, François?"

"Nothing, absolutely nothing."

"*I* see hell rising up from paradise. Hold me close, I don't love you, but I'm pretending that I love you."

François embraced her without saying a word. Suddenly, he began to cry. Sylvie did not know whether she was disgusted or moved. But she thought of the woman in the restaurant and she felt extremely uncomfortable.

"*I'm* not pretending anything," he said bitterly. "Marry me, Sylvie."

"I will never marry you," she replied, enunciating every syllable.

"Why?"

"Because I loathe chemistry and chemists' children and chemists' wives. Because I was born for something else."

"For what? For whom?"

"For me."

She clung closer to him. It meant almost nothing to her that he loved her. All she asked of him was to be a man, she wanted him to be violent, ravenous. What was he waiting for, to deliver her from this

82

desire? He pushed her away as she was kissing him with a kind of despairing passion.

"Why are you here, since you don't love me?"

She did not know what to answer. She had suddenly become aware that a certain physical ardour can produce the illusion of happiness.

He turned on the light and stood up, scowling.

"Your parents will be getting anxious, I must take you back. Anyway, you've made quite a big enough fool of me."

Her temples were throbbing painfully. Her drunkenness had evaporated.

"One doesn't make a fool of people by being honest with them. I've never lied to you."

"That's true."

As he was helping her into her coat, he clasped her once more in his arms. But he despised himself for this gesture. He had a feeling of impotent rage at the thought that, in spite of the romantic character of his relations with the black prince and the million francs he was going to earn every month, Sylvie only wanted him to be a faun or satyr.

She was almost asleep when he deposited her on her doorstep.

"My dear Claude,

Tonight I dreamt that I was dreaming of Éléonore. In my dream, I was trying to explain this

83

dream to her in which she was the moon, as frozen and insensible as the moon. She occupied the entire sky on a starless night. I was straining myself to find out why I was suffering so much, so as to be able to tell her, to write it to her one day.

I woke up in a kind of panic. Was it possible to suffer so much just in a dream?

As soon as I got up, I left the house and went to your room. The storm gave the roofs, grey in the mauve sky, a sombre, tragic look. Streets, houses, cowls and chimney-pots were no longer an urban landscape, but a stage-setting where I was waiting for the drama that I felt was inevitably going to be played out there. I waited and waited, but nothing happened. The tragedy was in myself. To avert it, I'm writing to you.

I've seen Albine and François. They have this in common: they don't question themselves about their reasons for acting. These seem to them as self-evident as their own existence. I didn't mention you to Albine.

Is your book progressing? I rather envy you. I sometimes have the feeling that I haven't the slightest reason for eating or sleeping or breathing. It seems to me that, if I had something to say, everything would take on a meaning. But I've no desire, like you, to go on indefinitely carping at the absurdity of life and of myself. In any case, I'm not at all convinced of the absurdity. Albine and

François are sufficient proof to me that one can be happy in a coherent world on condition that one cares about something. Even if it's only money. By using the most fantastic means, François is getting nearer every day to achieving the end he has set himself, which is to lord it over his grocer and his garage-proprietor and the local shopgirls with wads of banknotes. As for Albine, she dreams of nothing but a life of adventure, and thinks it the most sensible thing in the world to expose herself to the most senseless dangers.

Now and then one meets restless creatures of an even stranger race who want to be useful to their fellow-beings. They talk about their mission and, whether they are industrialists, teachers, doctors or politicians, atheists or fervent Christians, they believe they are clearly chosen by heaven to accomplish their task. I can't help regarding them as puppets worshipping their own strings. But, if you hold that kind of belief, it should be easy to live till you die of it. What else can I hope for, except to be like them one day?

Éléonore is definitely of that race. Yet what I admire in her is the energy and the unostentatious fervour she puts into accomplishing her dedicated task. I still cannot believe that she is going to sacrifice all the years that lie ahead of her to some sort of religious vocation. Sometimes I feel that I am here to catch hold of her skirt and restrain her by force from flying away from the sphere of her real life. But for some days I have had no strength, no voice. I want to beg her to come, but I daren't either write or telephone. And here I am back in your room, all alone, and fighting down the sudden impulse to cry.

Write to me often.

Sylvie."

That morning, as Sylvie was preparing once more to nourish herself on despair, the maid knocked at the door and handed her an express letter. She recognised the handwriting at once.

"Could you come to your beloved bar in the Rue Racine today, about 6.30? I shall be in the neighbourhood and would gladly meet you there. If I don't see you (it will be my fault for giving you such short notice) I will get in touch with you as soon as I see a chance of a free moment.

Hoping to see you today.

J. Blessner."

Sylvie read and re-read these words, stupefied. Was she enraptured or vaguely scandalised? Up till now, Julienne Blessner had remained on her guard. And

86

now she was taking the initiative and seeking a meeting . . .

All during the day, Sylvie could think of nothing but her astonishment. Something must have happened. Perhaps Julienne had discovered that God did not exist, that Mother Marie-Sainte-Cécile was only an old woman, that life still has some value when one is twenty-five. It was with a vague sense of triumph that she perched herself on one of the stools of her favourite bar, at twenty-five past six.

Julienne Blessner was a polite and punctual person. She arrived almost at once.

"I'm very glad to see you. I've been thinking about you so much."

"Thinking what?"

Julienne stared at her in surprise.

"Wondering what you were doing, whether you were still keeping up your work and . . . and giving me a thought now and then."

"I don't understand what you mean."

It was so easy to be cruel. Sylvie experienced a delicious feeling of revenge.

But Julienne did not allow herself to be upset.

"You understand perfectly. What have you been doing since we last saw each other?"

"Nothing."

This time Julienne was roused.

"Are you saying that simply to be disagreeable?"

"I'm saying it because it's true."

87

"Why are you so fond of creating negative situations?"

"I'm not creating anything. A week ago, anyone would have supposed you'd come simply to impress me with the fact that you couldn't be entirely at my beck and call. To make me realise it even more emphatically than by not coming. So that I shouldn't forget that you'd come from Sainte-Thérèse and were going back to Sainte-Thérèse. I promised you to work because of you, not because of Sainte-Thérèse. I've already told you I've no personal motive for passing exams I find utterly senseless. I shan't pass them."

"You promised me . . ."

"I promised you to work for a week, and I did so."

Julienne felt that her friendship was no longer anything but a spent, useless force.

"Then how do you get through your days?"

"Just as you're getting through that gin. They intoxicate me."

Julienne shrugged her shoulders.

"Now you're talking like a third-rate book. I don't like it."

"I'm not talking like a book. I spend the best part of my days here, and my nights, too, waiting for you."

"You knew perfectly well that I shouldn't come. Besides, you never told me that you were waiting for me."

"No. I was quite aware that you wouldn't come."

Common sense occasionally acts as an antidote to poison. Julienne refused to let herself be affected.

"If you persist in going on like this, I shall give up seeing you altogether."

But Sylvie pretended not to hear. She stared fixedly straight ahead, as if hope were still in the distance.

"All the same, I needed to see you," went on Julienne. "I need to be sure that you'll do what your parents and Mother Marie-Sainte-Cécile and I myself expect of you. There's no one who cares more about it than I do, Sylvie."

"You're wrong. I shan't do anything at all."

Sylvie ordered two more gin fizzes. One of the regular haunters of the bar came up and declared lyrically:

"I love you, as one loves the polka, the samba, the rumba."

"Go and love them somewhere else," said Sylvie savagely.

"Right, only come with me."

A student punched him on the shoulder. The man raised his cap and meekly slouched off.

The silence between Sylvie and Julienne hardened.

"What are you thinking about?" Sylvie asked at last.

Julienne remained as rigidly still as a figure in a

stained-glass window. After a moment, almost without moving her lips, she murmured:

"At the hold sin has over us."

Sylvie was swallowed up in amazement.

"I don't understand, I simply can't understand."

"*I* can't understand how you can like this place."

A strident laugh burst out at the other end of the bar. Julienne stood up.

"I ought not to have come."

She had stayed only a quarter of an hour. They parted, frozen in a mutual misunderstanding more intolerable than the fiercest enmity.

A fortnight went by. A fortnight of interminable days for Sylvie, who had been conscious every moment of an absence. She met friends, chance acquaintances, people who meant nothing to her. Those were the only people who existed now. Life was always on the other side, over the way, in other people's homes, elsewhere. Never had she been so keenly conscious of being nothing but an onlooker. Finally, Albine emerged from this blank anonymity.

"My uncle's written to me. He wants me to go and see him."

"With luck, you can get him under your thumb."

"How?"

"He's tired of existence. If you know how to amuse him, he's at your mercy."

"But why should he give in?"

"Because you're barely eighteen. If he's written to you, it's because he's got a kind of affection for you. Don't delude yourself, the old are only interested in us because they were once our age. We give them nostalgia. You represent what he can no longer attain."

"You think that, if I go and see him . . ."

"He'll say: 'When I was your age,' and he'll feel he's living all over again."

"It's so repulsive, an old man who can't do anything except get older! It's not even as if there were the slightest thing you could admire him for."

"Well, *we* haven't got to that stage yet. Personally, I have no intention of making old bones," exclaimed Sylvie. "I can't understand anyone daring to live after thirty."

"So what'll you do on your thirtieth birthday?"

"I shall kill myself."

"That's easily said."

"Let's make a pact to meet in thirteen years' time."

"All right, but only if we've failed. I promise you *I'm* not going to fail."

"And *I* promise you that I shall kill myself before I do."

They were prepared to challenge the impossible. Nevertheless, Sylvie had a foreboding that one grew older without noticing it.

To fail, or not to fail, but in what field? Was the

capturing of Julienne's attention the only thing to which she could aspire? Why were this love, this fervour, this frenzy and this bliss all that she pursued in this world?

It seemed to her that her own diary would finally reveal it to her one day.

3rd June.

I shall only discover my life through you, Julienne, and thanks to you. It's been said only too often that love is the main preoccupation of women. But, for me, love is you. What matters is not my overmastering passion, but what it implies. It is so real that, through you, I believe I discover more than Plato or Aristotle or Christ were able to communicate to their disciples. One is never the disciple of anyone except the person who reveals you to yourself. What is it, then, that you have to teach me? The love of life, certainly, but not just any love of just any life. Self-respect, or rather respect for what is worth cultivating in oneself. Tolerance, but a tolerance that never truckles with the truth; that, whatever the circumstances or whatever cowardly things you let yourself do, doesn't induce you to call black white; the love of good even when one is giving oneself up to evil. You intend to turn away from this world. But can you leave me abandoned on the shore?

Julienne was so little able to abandon her that, a few days later, Sylvie received another express letter.

"Will you wait in for me at your cousin's, tomorrow night, Wednesday, from 10.30 onwards? (Excuse the late hour . . .) If not, telephone me at 7.30 at Mol. 92.48.

Hoping to see you tomorrow,

J. Blessner."

There is no greater happiness than the anticipation of happiness. For then happiness and hope melt into one and sweep your heart away. Such suspense is at once blissful and dramatic. Even though one is not yet entitled to experience it, the joy is imagined so intensely that it submerges all reality.

That night, Sylvie hardly touched her dinner. Her mother had no sooner risen from the table than she rushed round to the Rue des Beaux-Arts. Her mind, her body, Claude's little room could no longer contain her. She was exploding.

"I shall fly into splinters, the house will dissolve into thin air, how shall I ever live till her arrival? She didn't hesitate to suggest meeting me here, and in the middle of the night. Why, why did she want to do something so incongruous, something that doesn't fit in at all with the regular Sainte-Thérèse time-table?"

93

Ten strokes reverberated somewhere in the neighbourhood, ten strokes of a hoarse bell.

"At this hour, my friends at Sainte-Thérèse are asleep. They don't hear the hours strike, they have nothing to hope from them. *I* am waiting for you, for *you*, my beloved. My life-pulse is only the beat of these passing moments."

When Julienne knocked at the door and the half-hour struck from the belfry, Sylvie barely had the strength to get up and draw back the bolt.

From the moment Julienne entered the room and the door closed behind her, Sylvie felt that she was someone else, someone she could only be in Julienne's presence. Normally she forgot that someone the moment Julienne had gone, but that night, when she found herself alone again, she felt the need to revive her in her journal.

18th June.

What I am, to become what I am. Perhaps you are only the pretext for that. If I truly love you, you and not myself, I have only to bow down before what makes your life. But I cannot forget that my life is involved, too. You were here just now, you are still here. Usually you leave me when you yourself are gone. Tonight I feel you with me, even more than just now. I know that, in thought, you are still here.

When you came in, Julienne, your face gave me

the impression that your coming here was a defeat for you rather than a joy. And I, who had been waiting for you with so much happiness, didn't dare to utter a word.

Julienne vanquished! I had never wanted that sort of victory.

I watched her walk across the room, sit down, get up and start walking again. All at once, she burst out:

'This situation is becoming intolerable. I cannot bear to imagine you in process of destroying yourself, I loathe the world you are living in, I loathe imagining you in it. Is it possible that we have nothing more to say to each other, that, in expelling you from Sainte-Thérèse, they have really expelled you from the only world that seems rational to me? Can our lives have become so utterly far apart?'

She went on pacing up and down. I remained silent. I knew very well that our souls, if not our lives, were anything but far apart. I say our souls, because one has to give a name to something that is implied in a look and revealed in a tone of voice, something that is enough to disrupt one's whole life.

'The only world that seems rational to her . . .'

Didn't she realise, then, that she carries that world in herself, and that it isn't necessary, as she keeps insisting more and more every day, to confine it to the enclosure of a convent, particularly of the convent of Sainte-Thérèse? Obviously, I couldn't

95

follow her into that. I didn't even succeed in remaining in it.

She began to talk again.

'It's unthinkable that, because of me, because you have had to leave school on my account, you should give up the idea of passing an exam that may be vitally important to you one day. I can't possibly allow that. I'm asking you, I'm begging you to promise me that you're not only going to work, but going to succeed.'

She was talking like the worst kind of solicitor's wife. I remained more firmly resolved than ever not to pass my Baccalaureate. *I* don't ever intend to be a solicitor, or a solicitor's wife, either. I would have gladly offered her my life, my soul, my eternal salvation, but I could not make her the promise she asked of me. I would have needed an essential, personal reason, not a sentimental one to go on playing at mathematics and natural science and everything I find even more boring than a card-game I don't want to play.

'I promise you that the day I'm convinced I've really got to work, I will work. But I'm not going to do it just to collect diplomas.'

She tried to explain to me that diplomas were indeed nothing, but that it was a good thing for a woman who would one day choose a profession, or a cultured man as a husband, to have a trained mind, an academic polish, a form of mental armour.

Luckily, I wasn't listening to her. In any case, that was not exactly what she said, but it was how I should have interpreted it if I had been trying to understand.

I was listening so little or so badly that Julienne stopped talking. Silence descended between us like twilight. Had we really nothing more to say to each other? We stared at each other in terror, our minds and hearts buzzing with futile words. But our looks said clearly enough that the essence of our conversation remained unspoken.

'Julienne . . .'

'No, don't say anything. I know.'

She did not dare look at me.

I tried, with everything in me that is best and frankest and most worthy of her, to find words she would listen to.

'Julienne, this time you won't have to regret having come. Only leave the choice of means to me. Don't forget that, for me, you are a model. If you turn away from the world, I shall find myself back in the desert.'

She thrust out her hand, as if pushing away my last words.

'I'm anything but a model. And if I do turn away from the world, perhaps then, and then only, I shall turn towards what, for me, is *the* model.'

'What is that?'

'The example of detachment and love.'

97

'Love and detachment? I don't understand how the two can go together. If God created the world, why should he demand that people should detach themselves from it?'

'I don't know.' From the tone of her voice, I knew that nothing could be more shattering to her than such an admission. 'It's not for us to question ourselves about God's demands.'

'But, after all, what do you call love? I love you, Julienne, and you mean to destroy that love . . . At least, the nuns mean to. We're told we've got to love our neighbour as ourselves, and when, for once, we think we've at last managed to do it, we're commanded to renounce this much-vaunted love and put an end to it.'

'Our neighbour can't be just one single person.'

'And suppose only one single person could reveal to you what was up to then only a dead letter?'

'You mix everything up.'

'When I look at you, I'm convinced that I experience love more deeply and fully than any of *them* can, all your charitable ladies and your Mother Marguerite-Maries and your priests.'

'The day you manage to love priests and ragamuffins and charitable ladies like that, the day you no longer reject anyone, you'll know better than I do what love is. I've strained with all my heart towards that, but so far in vain.'

'And the tribe of female Christians flaps its wings, crying love, love.'

'What's that you're saying?'

'Nothing. A quotation from Montherlant. A writer your nuns don't always appreciate.'

Had I insulted her? She stood up, her face darkened.

'We definitely can't understand each other. The most we can do is . . ."

'Love each other!'

For a moment, I thought, insanely, that she was going to say yes.

She ran her hand over her face.

'Don't force me never to see you again.'

She put on her coat. She did it out of duty, I could feel that.

'I'm not forcing you to do anything. You know very well that, where you're concerned, my whole life is one long waiting.'

She opened the door, and, in a voice I had never heard before, giving me a look that dazzled me, she said:

'I shall come back.'

I was incapable of making a movement, even of seeing her to the door, even of shutting it after her. I do not know whether she left an hour ago or a few minutes or an eternity. I only know that she is still here and that she will go on being here till she returns.

It was almost summer. It was summer. In the evening the pallor of the sky held back the night. It is wise to love only in winter. Spring and summer are accomplices. They invest desires with a halo of light.

Julienne was present in every second; Sylvie could never keep her out of her mind. Nevertheless, the days flew past. But all they carried away was an excess of time, an excess of life, hours that meant nothing. Before Sylvie had become conscious of the calendar, Julienne Blessner invited her one afternoon to meet her in the garden of the Palais-Royal. It was a journey to a foreign land. Sylvie's only haunts were the Luxembourg and the cemetery of Montparnasse—or, rather, the plots where the dead were adorned with flowers.

Why the Palais-Royal? Julienne explained that she felt at home there. The thought of Julienne in a short skirt, trotting along behind a hoop, took Sylvie straight back to the world of the Comtesse de Ségur, the world of little girls in crinolines and pantalettes. The old ladies who emerge in summer, who live all the year behind closed windows and only manifest their existence on June afternoons, arrived with measured steps. Sylvie inwardly thanked these innocent chaperons.

"You'll come back tomorrow, won't you, Julienne?"

"I'll come back."

So, day after day, long before sunset, they met under the arcades. They had nothing to say to each other. Only to live an hour. It is impossible to describe that garden, that hour, that day and the days that followed. They were made up of nothing but a little happiness. By mutual consent, Sylvie and Julienne avoided everything that might separate them.

Why, in summer, do there always have to be storms? The date of the Baccalaureate was approaching, and Julienne felt bound to mention it. Sylvie promptly backed away.

"I just don't understand your passion for ignorance," exclaimed Julienne, genuinely disheartened.

"There's no earthly point in my doing theorems and Latin proses. You've told me yourself that, for anyone who isn't going to need them in their profession, they're only an exercise. You know that I performed this exercise quite efficiently as long as school life was *my* life, as long as I hadn't been expelled from its discipline. That life finished for me three months earlier than it was expected to. I shan't find myself any the worse for that in twenty-five years' time. The exercise has come to an end. Let's say I've already turned over the page. What do I care about an official certificate to solemnise my farewell to the thing that had sustained me for so many years?"

Julienne stared at the gravel at her feet as if she were trying to find patterns in it.

"Did you like school?" she said at last.

Sylvie hesitated. Could she admit that, after having so much hated the stick-in-the-mud mentality of most of the nuns, she felt a sharp pang every time she thought of the classrooms from which she had been exiled?

"It was a kind of enchantment," she said, dreaming aloud. "The days were planned for you according to an inexorable rule. Every hour there had a particular savour, made up of imprisonment and companionship and emulation. You always felt you had to give something of yourself, not your heart, but everything that was strongest in your mind and character. Even if it was only to find the rude retort that would get you kept in on Sunday, or its opposite, the observation that would get you a few more good marks. I think the army prolongs that situation for men. For me, it will never be reproduced.

"I've known that kind of nostalgia," said Julienne, using that last word hesitantly, as if she feared a rebuff from Sylvie. "Perhaps that's why I was so happy to be admitted to Sainte-Thérèse."

"By the other door," said Sylvie, with a smile.

"If you like, but it shuts you in to the same discipline. The teacher is just as much tied down to it as the pupils in front of her."

Sylvie seemed sceptical. For her, teachers were inevitably a race whom pupils—and, in spite of what

102

she had just said, she still felt herself a pupil—longed, with rare exceptions, to see burning at the stake. Julienne realised, with a certain annoyance, that the eight years that separated her from Sylvie put a wider gulf between them than all the years that might stretch between herself and the oldest of the nuns. Suddenly, she was no longer Julienne Blessner, brought close to Sylvie Ceyvenole by their friendship and the sweetness of this June afternoon, but Mademoiselle Blessner, former schoolmistress of a seventeen-year-old girl who had got to pass her Baccalaureate.

"That life that you seem to regret," she said in a firm voice, "why don't you preserve the essential part of it by keeping up your studies?"

"What studies?"

"That, my dear Sylvie, is something you must discover for yourself."

"I quite agree. Only I haven't discovered it. In any case, as far as I know, a student's life bears no resemblance whatever to the life one may lead from childhood to adolescence. If it's true that I feel a certain regret, perhaps it's only regret for being at the age when one begins to run to seed."

"Sure enough, it's at fifteen and again at seventeen that one feels oneself getting older in a really agonising way. But when you no longer have to keep getting new shoes or new clothes because last year's have grown too small, you'll find that you'll have a feeling of stability that is quite pleasurable. When you've passed the age of discoveries and revelations, you reach the age of accomplishment."

Sylvie did not answer. She was feeling mildly bored.

"An illusory stability," Julienne went on, as if she were talking to herself. "But most people let themselves be taken in by it."

Sylvie stared at the clouds chasing each other and interlacing in the sky. Julienne became aware that she was not attending.

"Don't you understand, Sylvie, that your awkward age, your wild enthusiasms, your anxieties are only there to lead you on to a way of life that you can't just leave to chance? Make the effort to pass your exams, not to close your school career but so that all the doors will be open to you till you make up your mind which one you want to go through."

"If, at the age of thirty, I need the Baccalaureate in order to do something I've set my heart on, very well, I'll work for it at thirty."

"You know perfectly well that you'll no longer have either the capacity or the courage. You'll have long ago forgotten what examiners demand of candidates."

"But who says I'll ever want or need to pass this accursed 'Bac'? I'm certainly not going to force myself to do it out of prudence, like taking out an insurance policy. I've told you I won't pass it and I'm not going back on that."

"What will your parents think?"

Sylvie remained speechless. It was quite certain that Monsieur Ceyvenole would never allow her to escape the June session.

She evaded the question by asking one in her turn:

"Why are you so keen on my passing this exam?"

Julienne Blessner felt that her answer justified, once and for all, her feelings for Sylvie and the fact that, for some time, she had been seeing her every day.

"Because I want you to make a good use of your life. I shouldn't be here if your success didn't mean a great deal to me."

"There are other ways of succeeding besides . . ."

"What other ways?" Julienne interrupted, with obvious impatience.

Sylvie could only remain silent. Behind her obstinate expression, she was conscious of a dull sense of frustration. Not for anything in the world would she have been willing to admit that she was searching vainly, desperately, how to justify her existence. Only Claude could have been some help to her then by bursting out laughing at the words success and justification. But Julienne was not the woman to appreciate Claude's laughter. Sylvie chose bad temper.

"I'm certain nobody ever asked Eva Peron or Sarah Bernhardt or Charlotte Corday whether they'd passed their Baccalaureate."

"Is Charlotte Corday really one of your heroines?"

"It's not given to everyone to dare to commit a great crime. However, to be truthful, there are women whose daring I admire even more—the beautiful anarchists who shrank from nothing, not even robbery, to give a good example."

"I'm sorry, I can't see anything in all this but a lot of childishness."

It did not occur to Sylvie to be annoyed. She was too fond of Julienne's velvety laugh to be shocked to hear it, even at her own expense.

"The fact is," Julienne went on, in an almost harsh voice, "I'm beginning to think that you're trying to throw a romantic halo over a kind of cowardice and incapacity. You wouldn't hesitate to sit for this exam if you felt capable of passing it."

Sylvie was prepared to defy common sense, prudence, her father's anger and the opinion of all her friends, but not to incur Julienne's contempt. She clenched her fists, gritted her teeth, stood up and announced in a toneless voice:

"Right. I'll fail, but in my own way. I'll do it in such a manner that you won't be able ever, ever again to speak to me as you've done just now."

Without giving Julienne time to utter a word, she

walked off with rapid, angry steps and returned home as if she were going into battle.

"If Mademoiselle Blessner telephones," she told her mother, before shutting herself up in her room, "tell her that I'm working, and that I shan't be visible until after the Baccalaureate."

Her mother's look of happy surprise filled her with remorse. She threw her arms round her with the lovingness of a guilty child.

"Don't give yourself any illusions, I shan't pass. But, if you really love me, you mustn't be cross with me about it. I only ask you one thing, let me shut myself up in my room till the day of this exam."

"What crazy thing are you proposing to do now?" asked Madame Ceyvenole anxiously.

"A crazy thing that will prevent me from hating myself," replied Sylvie in a tone so bitter and resolute that her mother did not dare question her further.

There were ten days left before the ordeal of the Baccalaureate. Sylvie had always been first in French, unequal in mathematics, Latin and English. She brought out her exercise-books and text-books, calculated that, during these ten days, she would allow herself an average of four hours' sleep a night, and established her plan of campaign. She got her parents to allow her to have her meals served in her room.

By working eighteen hours a day, she would give herself enough time to revise everything she had learnt or refused to learn in the course of the past year.

It was not long before, to keep up with her time-table, she found it necessary to dope herself. She was amazed to discover the marvellous exaltation that benzedrine and similar drugs induce in those who employ them for heroic ends, who passionately use up the energy provided by a few pills. The less she slept, the less she ate, the more her mind felt alive and insatiable. She had already revised the curriculum of an entire term in a few days, when Albine forced her way in, despite the orders Sylvie had given her parents, and burst into her bedroom.

"Sorry, but I simply couldn't be so wildly happy without coming to tell you about it. My uncle's promised to finance the whole expedition if Ginette Collard will take me with her!"

While Albine was describing the old man's surrender and the curiosity and senile amusement his niece's enthusiasm for her plans had aroused, Sylvie was conscious of a dull, but persistent ache in the region of her heart as if something were pinching it. Albine had won, Albine knew what she wanted, Albine was even suggesting that she should go off with her. Yet she had not the least desire to cross jungles or steppes or even deserts, to join caravans, to watch lamas at prayer, to hear cracked, twanging music. Then what did she desire, what did she want? The impossible, but an impossibility so vast and diffused that she could not grasp it. For the moment, she was achieving what she wanted by learning her courses in algebra and geometry and English by heart, and going over every fair copy of a Latin prose she had ever made.

"I'll leave you to your scholastic frenzy," said Albine, with a smile. "But in a fortnight's time I'll come and see you again, and then I hope to persuade you to come with me."

That evening, Sylvie had considerable difficulty in concentrating on her work. She felt as if she were struggling against the night without knowing what the dawn would bring, without knowing what she could expect from the day and all the days that would follow. She fell asleep lying face-down on her bed, with her head on a dictionary. When she woke up, long before her alarm clock had gone off, the sky was already the colour of milk. One could hear heavy lorries rumbling along the boulevard, but bourgeois cars and bourgeois pedestrians had not ventured out on it yet. Sylvie had not undressed; she went over to the window and opened it wide as if she could have dived through it into the sky. She took long, deep breaths and gazed at the row of houses on the opposite pavement, in the pale, washed-out glimmer that preceded the light. She remembered the Utrillo exhibition she had seen with

Claude, a week before his departure. All the boulevards, all the fronts of the houses had looked to her like that. Would she have ever seen the houses as she was seeing them now, if she had not gone to that exhibition? Every time she had steeped herself in the world of a painter, she had discovered that world in everything about her, for days, sometimes for weeks afterwards.

But when the trees had lost the memory of Van Gogh and the houses had forgotten Utrillo, would a personal world of her own never be born? Ever since Adam and Eve, hadn't the world been given to every man and every woman, as often as a man or a woman appeared on earth to contemplate it?

It was Sunday. People were beginning to set off to Mass. It had begun to rain, some puddles had formed. The atmosphere of that particular Sunday morning impinged on her like the smell of hot rolls. Whether it was lack of sleep, the effect of stimulants or simply a special grace, Sylvie became more conscious every moment of the extraordinary actuality of things. People no longer appeared to her as interchangeable, anonymous beings, they were definitely that respectably-dressed, pot-bellied gentleman who was lighting a cigar, that woman in black hurrying across the Rue Vavin and stepping aside on the pavement to avoid a puddle. The man, the woman, the puddle, each one had a language, the language of their irreplaceable existence. If she could express that, or draw that! Perhaps the emotion she had just begun to feel, the entirely fresh look she was casting on the street, were nothing exceptional for an artist who remains, without knowing it, and with the utmost simplicity, in a constant state of grace. Was that possible? Did artists never, like herself, feel as dull as a civil servant longing only for his retirement? But this particular day, to hell with civil servants! For the past few minutes, she had been wanting to push aside Utrillo and Dufy and Van Gogh and describe all this in her own way—this Paris street, so provincial at this early hour, the woman in black, the man with the cigar, the aroma of Mass and of Sunday that pervaded it all.

She seized a pencil. An aroma of Mass and of Sunday, an aroma of Mass and of Sunday, she kept saying to herself as, with big, sweeping strokes she drew the sky and the puddle, expressing all she could of the way she saw them.

"I don't know how to draw, but if I went to school, to a school where at least I'd be taught what I need to learn, couldn't I impose my own vision, explore the world, seize the passing moment? Julienne, don't you realise that, for me, that would be gaining something far more important than a Baccalaureate that leads to nothing?"

She was pacing up and down the room. The boulevard, the puddle, this royal gift of a morning had gone to her head. Suddenly, she planted herself in front of the window and shouted to the sky, where the light was now growing: "I swear to astound myself!"

Then she flung herself on her bed and slept till noon.

The first examination for the Baccalaureate took place three days later. Sylvie had only left off working to go round to the Secretary's office at the École des Beaux-Arts where they had confirmed her belief that she did not need to pass her Baccalaureate in order to be allowed to take the entrance exam. She had returned home, announced the joyful news to her parents and asked their blessing, in other words their permission to enter for this exam, and got down to work again. She slept only three hours a night. The morning she presented herself in the examination hall, she could flatter herself that she had entirely re-read and practically learnt by heart the contents of her English, Latin and mathematical text-books.

"I'm going to astonish Julienne," she sang inwardly, while they were handing out paper and the list of subjects for the French Essay. The last one made her start.

"Using Baudelaire's sonnet, *Correspondances*, as your basis, discuss, illustrating your theme with concrete and personal examples, whether the poet's knowledge of nature is deeper than that of the scientist."

"I say, what a marvellous subject!" she said aloud, much to the scandal of her neighbour, who put out her tongue. But her resolution was taken and there was no going back on it. She would fail, she would throw away the only good marks that seemed easy to obtain; she would deliberately set out to get zero for the very subject in which Julienne and the whole of Sainte-Thérèse were hoping to see her shine. On the other hand, she would make short work of the papers at which Julienne expected her to blench.

No doubt, she was indulging in a good many illusions. Having only three hours' sleep a night for ten days is not enough to make a person good at book-learning or turn them into a first-class mathematician. But she was at the age when the wings of imagination carry one far, and when sometimes one has only to have a firm faith in impossibilities to bring them within one's reach. With her cheeks hollow from lack of sleep and her eyelids burning, she was as confident of her luck as of her ability.

She considered the subject for a moment. It would not have displeased her to wrestle with it, compose her thoughts into an orderly sequence, launch out into a thousand paradoxes that would cunningly lead to a rational conclusion. She shook her head, like a snarling puppy. It was not that she was weakening. For a moment, she thought of getting up and handing in a blank sheet of paper. But she found the subject decidedly inspiring. Why should she deny herself the pleasure of talking about it in another language? She took up her pencil and began to draw areas and zones, lakes cr steppes that corresponded to each other without merging into each other. "Abstract Essay" she wrote solemnly. She was so engrossed that she did not see the invigilator's gaze dwelling on her.

"What's that you're doing?" a sharp, indignant voice asked abruptly.

"Illustrating correspondences," replied Sylvie, completely unmoved.

She handed him her sheet of paper and left the hall slowly and with dignity.

She lived through the days that followed in a state half-way between a dream and a nightmare. She had the feeling that she was pouring out ten days of her life and seventeen years of energy on to the sheets of paper they put in front of her. She gritted her teeth so hard that, from time to time, she put a finger in her mouth to relax herself. But she wrote down words and figures that she understood. Now and then, everything became blurred. However, her memory did not fail, and she had enough intelligence to use it. She was triumphing but, as it seemed to her, at the price of her blood. She could feel it throbbing in her temples, harassing her heart. Julienne would never suspect that, for her sake, she had passed through the ordeal of fire, the fire of passion and pride. She would be modest in her triumph. She would simply say: "Look, I've got a zero in French, a twelve in mathematics, a fourteen in English and Latin."

She managed, by the skin of her teeth, to get ten and eleven. But she had got through the ordeal and she felt that, for the rest of her life, she would be able to look herself in the face. The years to come mattered little, too, she was wildly conscious of having acquired the right to paint her life all colours of the rainbow at the Beaux-Arts or elsewhere. Now she had only one thought, to sleep and to capture Julienne.

She slept for nearly twenty-four hours, then for fifteen, then for twelve, waking up and going to sleep again in a rapture of bliss. Julienne telephoned almost every day, morning and evening. She did not speak to her till she was in a position to tell her her marks. Then she savoured a moment of rare intensity; the silence and stupefaction of Julienne. Almost at once, her joy was dissipated. Julienne had hung up without saying a word.

The following morning, the post brought a letter from Claude.

"Dear Sylvie, I am suffering a thousand deaths. I no longer live except to scribble a few pages and

I cannot believe that I have produced such a mass of words. What's become of Albine? Sometimes I catch myself thinking that I love her like a dying man too much in love with life. Her hardness, her elegance haunt me as a spring obsesses a man lost in the Sahara. The provinces are totally devoid of anyone like Albine. She is only imaginable in Paris or Tibet, although my obsession convinces me that she would only have to appear to transfigure the provinces. Tell me about her, tell me about yourself.

I am vainly trying to force myself to get on with this book I am writing, and which I feel as if I were murdering. It will take hardly more than fifty pages to finish it, yet I know I shan't need as many as that before I begin to laugh. For what I am writing is nothing but a reflection of myself. Inevitably I express what I have lived, while pretending to give these pages a universal and sententious character. But how can one catch oneself at one's own game? Perhaps, to tell the truth, all that doesn't exist. So many images, so many faces that I have done no more than touch, or occasionally scratch, or implore, so many scattered names, so many rash thoughts. Weren't they all there only to prove that I am completely alone, or had they another meaning? Love, friendship, solitude themselves seem to me illusions. All the same, I think of you often and, misanthrope that I am, this thought is dear to me.

You haven't written to me for a very long time. No doubt it's the fault of the Baccalaureate. What did you make of it?

Answer quickly.

Claude."

Claude must come back to Paris, Sylvie kept telling herself. He's vegetating, he's mouldering, he'll die for lack of oxygen. Filled with a sense of responsibility, she set about answering him.

"I've failed in the Baccalaureate to do you honour and to startle Julienne. For ten days, I lived for nothing but to triumph over mathematics, English and Latin, taking good care to win a zero for French. What do you think of that? It seems to me that you can only approve. But please, please, come and tell me so. Besides, Albine haunts you, come and pluck her. She doesn't love you, you know that. All the same, you are one of the very few young men she chooses to admire. I should have thought it didn't need more than that to conquer a girl. But, for goodness' sake, love her for herself. She is the exact opposite of you. She doesn't care in the least whether things have or haven't a meaning, she only lives to go prancing about. In a few weeks, she'll be on her

117

way to the Indies, and that road will only lead her to other roads that she'll never get tired of roving. In her eyes, you embody the faculty she most completely lacks, the ability to think. I think that if you were less of a fool, in other words, less sensitive, you could easily dazzle her.

I've only the vaguest idea what your book is about, but I'm sure it's just a collection of recipes for madness and non-living. Personally, I prefer madness. I failed in the Baccalaureate, when I'd done everything possible to get myself up to scratch to pass, simply and solely because I refused to make a normal, bourgeois gesture. I've decided to go to the Beaux-Arts and learn to paint, and I've verified that you don't need the Baccalaureate to get in. This prudence proves that I'm only your cousin, not your double. I can't understand your taking such pleasure in annihilating yourself when you only need a little guts to come back to Paris and Albine.

Baci.

Sylvie."

Before sticking down the envelope, Sylvie forced herself to stop and think. Wasn't the last sentence too harsh? She was fond enough of Claude to risk it. She stuck down the envelope.

She received an answer by return of post.

"Dear lunatic, ought I to congratulate you on your latest exploit? I think it wiser to admire the decision you have so *prudently* made, to go to the Beaux-Arts without bothering to acquire your 'bac'.

Your last letter, my love, inspires me with profound respect. It even has a patronising tone: 'If you had a little more "guts" ' . . . And what should I do if I had? I should almost certainly be devoured by ambition, if this exalted passion did not inevitably have to be exercised among men. But my personal ambition is to do without them, to forget them, to forget myself. I care no more about conquering Paris than about conquering Albine. I am simply suffering from a weakness for both of them. But, in the inmost depths of myself, I feel stripped of that weakness. It even seems to me that, ever since I've been producing a book, I've been stripping myself of my own personality. Like a tree slowly losing its leaves, I see my joys and sorrows and hopes vanishing. I've reached the point where I can no longer stand anything or anyone.

To love others, one must first love oneself. I cannot see anything admirable about being a mechanism more or less efficiently wound up for a period of X years. One can only experience the satisfaction of delighting in oneself on condition that one plays the game of life.

I cannot.

But I can still love you, my rare bird—no doubt

it's my last privilege—and I'll come and see you
soon.

Claude."

In its own way, this letter was a huge satisfaction
to Sylvie. All the same, even as she was toying with
the envelope, she began to dream of another handwriting, a more compact and disciplined one, that
she thought must inevitably appear. She only waited
eight days for its appearance.

"We are so different that it surprises me now that
any kind of friendship could have been established
between us. What you have just done is contrary to
everything I felt I had the right to expect of you. I
shall never understand what pride, what vanity, what
coquetry led you to do it. I am forced to admit to myself that my friendship has no effect on you, that you
can do without it. Don't be surprised if you never see
me again. What need is there for you to see me? You
lead your life in your own way, and I have always had
a profound respect for the choice, the decisions and
the liberty of other people. But there comes a moment
when, however much one respects these things, one
fails to understand them. At that point it is better to
withdraw oneself. I wish you many successes in your
chosen field of activity, if possible for a less

disconcerting kind than the one you were pleased to offer me.

J. Blessner."

Sylvie could have jumped for joy. Julienne annoyed! That was a hitherto unknown aspect of her. The thing now was to write her a breathless, stunning letter, full of appeasing incense.

"Julienne, how am I to write to you? I know that you reject words and that, in your eyes, anything one believes one has grasped and retained, in other words formulated, is valueless. Yet I would like to be able to offer you a few full-stops, commas and semicolons. It isn't true that I have dispossessed myself of you. Quite the reverse. Either I am nothing but an illusion of myself or else I was on the point of attaining, through you, my truest reality. This voyage of discovery began at Sainte-Thérèse, it has continued right up to this Baccalaureate that was my salvation. I met you at the moment when I was on the verge of abandoning everything. You made me realise that success matters, but not official success, the kind that consecrates you in the eyes of other people. Was *that* what you expected of me? Don't you realise that there were only two people to whom I had to render accounts—yourself and myself?

How I've come to feel more definitely what I want to be, at rock-bottom, is something I shall only know if you don't take fright. The road is still slippery for me. I live in a universe that is becoming less blurred, but that perhaps will never be fixed. I haven't yet quite emerged from a fog, and even the fact of having been able to pierce it has left me stunned. For a long time, my only effort has been to try and see clear through it, as far as I possibly could.

I want to paint, I don't quite know why. I shall only discover that by actually painting. Julienne, it's I who am going to the Beaux-Arts now. I want you there with me. Because I met you when I was in utter confusion, because I expected you to give me the key to mysteries and to certainties, you took me by the hand. Now I feel everything is getting clearer. But what barriers are you going to set up against me? Am I going to knock my head up once more against your life of *credos* and virtues?

Come and see me.

Sylvie."

The following morning, Sylvie received a card bearing these words: "Half-past two."

Without losing a moment, Sylvie rushed off to the Rue des Beaux-Arts. Much as she loathed doing it, she cleaned up the room, then went out and bought some flowers. These gestures seemed to her absurdly conventional, but she did not want the dust to be held against her. It was half-past one; she had eaten hastily, and very little at that. She stretched herself on the divan and, until half-past two, lay there with her eyes shut and her jaws clenched.

She did not hear Julienne knock. The key was on the outside of the door, which opened softly.

"I'm so sorry, I'm afraid I've woken you up."

"I never sleep. No, don't laugh, I dream and it's always of you."

"I haven't come here to listen to a lot of nonsense."

Julienne Blessner sat down and, for some moments, was nothing but a sphinx. On Sylvie, her visit produced the effect of a waking dream. She preserved the memory of it:

3rd July.

Julienne appeared to me like a frightened ghost. Yet we were in broad daylight. Anyone would have supposed that I terrified her.

'What is it you hope from me?' she said at last.

Everything, nothing—what could I answer? I had the feeling of having engaged in a contest where the stake was much more than love, much more than happiness, the very foundations of my life.

123

'I want you to come with me, I want to meet you in the corridors when I go to the Beaux-Arts, I want . . .'

'You want to substitute your life for mine.'

'No, I don't, But I do believe our destinies are parallel. Otherwise, Julienne, why would you be here?'

Silence can sometimes be so heavy that it has all the weight of an accusation, an admission, an overwhelming piece of evidence. Julienne never speaks when she has nothing to say. It was perfectly clear that she could not be anywhere else. Suddenly, I felt the urge to stand up, to make a speech to her, to convince her, to catch her out. Did I talk, did I dream? I don't know. She never took her eyes off me. I know nothing about happiness and yet I seem to have defended it fiercely.

I told her endlessly over and over again that I adored her, insisting on that word one uses only for God, till I made her shudder. I did not let her get in one word.

'Can't one believe in the reality of something that is only fleeting, the reality of happiness for example? To prefer an imperishable bliss to happiness in this perishable world as you claim to do, isn't that just simply preferring it didn't exist?'

I talked and I talked. I could see her growing smaller before my eyes, losing ground, flinching. For a long time, I thought she was no longer listening to me. I was cruelly conscious of this zone of absence, this space between oneself and what one loves, oneself and the person one values most. Yet every silence, every breath, brought her closer to me.

'What is it you want, Sylvie?'

'I want you to leave Sainte-Thérèse. Thursday, at two o'clock, I shall wait for you outside the secretary's room at the École des Beaux-Arts so that you can enrol along with me.'

She did not protest. I foresaw her possible fall and I took a bitter pleasure in it.

'Say something, Julienne. Tell me whether I'm right or I'm wrong.'

'I should have told you long ago if I'd been certain either way.'

'Why hesitate so much?'

She did not answer. But she left the armchair where she had been sitting, as if wedged into it, and came and sat on the bed beside me. For the space of a second, she closed her eyes.

'I ought not to be here,' she said at last. 'When one has made one's choice, one ought to stick to it. But I cannot make up my mind to . . .'

"She did not finish her sentence. I finished it for her.

'To destroy us?'

How futile words were! I had taken her hand and, as I held it almost at the height of the wrist, I

125

could feel her blood racing between my fingers. I think that I made the gesture of kneeling down.

'Julienne, I want . . .'

Like someone warding off danger, she cried out: 'Don't speak!' But her eyes could not tear themselves away from mine.

I did not embrace her. Will she ever forgive me for that? Too much love kills love. A worshipper cannot bring himself to blaspheme; I remained petrified, vanquished. She did not belong to me, she belonged to Sainte-Thérèse, under the blue mantle of the Blessed Virgin, on an invisible pedestal that removed her from me. How could I do anything but kneel? Should I have loved her if she'd been the kind of woman one takes in one's arms?

I do not remember how she left. Certainly neither of us uttered a word. My silence was sufficient admission of my defeat, an admission that there are people whom one cannot break. Whether or not one believes in God, there are moments when He suddenly rises up like a rampart. Yet it is not He, directly, who impresses me so much in Julienne, but that loftiness He has given her, that integrity. In most Christians, God appears to me as a scarecrow. He makes them timorous, petty. In Julienne, He shines. Unless my love confuses the two and He has nothing to do with it.

I went to bed utterly dazed and desperately unhappy.

126

On Thursday, at two o'clock, Sylvie paced up and down in front of the École des Beaux-Arts, but with no hope. The pavement, the street, the sky were nothing to her but a cage from which she felt she would never escape: the world without Julienne; life, her whole life without Julienne. She went on waiting. She waited till three o'clock, till four o'clock. This waiting, she was convinced, would be her last contact with Julienne. When she returned home and the concierge handed her a letter, she waited a long time more, pointlessly, before opening it. She had imagined only one single sentence: "I do not want to see you." This letter told her so in a page.

"It is impossible for me to renounce my life-long striving towards light, truth and simplicity. In so far as I set aside this aim, I suffer profoundly; I am no longer myself.

You will soon discover that you no longer need me. And you will forgive me for dedicating myself entirely to what, for me, is Life. It is better, for both of us, to stop seeing each other.

Soon, I shall be entering on my novitiate. I shall think of you very often. Be sure of that, and be sure, too, that only prayer can unite the two of us in the best and truest part of ourselves.

Sylvie, do go and see Mother Marie-Sainte-Cécile.

127

She will speak to me of you as in future I'd want you to be spoken of and I hope I shall hear from her that at last you are devoting yourself to something worth doing. Work, pass your entrance to the Beaux-Arts. When you are there, you will discover that beautiful things are simple; that is the first principle of art: it does not lie. Perhaps you will also discover that this principle can lead direct to God.

I ask you only one favour: don't write to me any more. But do not lose confidence, I shall be with you in thought—always.

Your
Julienne."

It was the first time Julienne Blessner had signed one of her letters with her Christian name. Sylvie repeated that name endlessly, over and over again, sobbing.

7th July.
I cannot believe it and yet I know that it is true. Through my own fault, because I didn't dare make her step down from her pedestal, I have lost Julienne. I've driven her into this novitiate, I've dedicated her to the convent. Yet never have I loved her more. I keep repeating St. Augustine's cry: 'Oh,

the madness of not knowing how to love men as men!' and it acquires a meaning for me that the author of the *Confessions* certainly did not intend: I did not dare make the gesture that would have restored Julienne to life, that would have given her to me. I cannot imagine the days going on and on without her, and yet I know that it cannot be otherwise. Would my heart burn so fiercely if it were not devoured by the impossible? Where did I get this passion for the impossible that has always made me neglect the possible? Julienne has broken with me yet she could not have imprisoned me more completely. Now I am locked up in the absolute of this forbidden love. I shall never be cured of it. I am caught in a spell, bewitched. I want to die, to die of love, to exhaust all the oxygen in my lungs, to burn like a torch. She is everything to me. Never shall I be able to go on living without seeing her, without writing to her. I shall extinguish myself like the fire when one smothers it. Julienne, Julienne, Julienne, Julienne. Do not deprive me of myself.

Albine tried in vain to see Sylvie. She was longing to tell her about the preparations for the expedition, and to persuade her to join it. Sylvie told her family to tell Albine that she was ill and could see no one. It was true. Nevertheless, she wrote to Claude. Paradoxically, he appeared to her as a last resort against the despair he was always extolling.

10th July.

"Claude, please, come back. You've lost Albine, I've lost Éléonore, but it was not the same love. You are to Éléonore what night is to day. Come back: I need the night.

You will jeer at God, you will jeer at me and at yourself. And we'll laugh about it together. Yet no one will know better than you that we are jeering at the light.

I want to read your book. I forbid you to ridicule it. Perhaps, indeed only too probably, I shall only make horrible daubs with my paintbrush. A Sunday painter . . . But I shan't despise my Sunday efforts. If I fail, it will not be for want of having loved a dream!

Nevertheless, I am completely stunned. For me, Éléonore was the incarnation of all that love. She was my bulwark. Shall I ever be able to face the Beaux-Arts without her, my life without her? You might as well ask me to paint without colours, to dream without dreams, to live without life. What am I to do?

Claude, come back! You'll bring its old dusty, nocturnal smell back to your room. Bring Albine back your love, bring me the magic of your laugh. You can laugh at death with impunity. You know how to laugh.

I beg you to come back to me.

Sylvie."

130

Claude came back. He was not one of those who refuse their help. But it seemed odd to him having to persuade Sylvie that it was possible to live, even without Éléonore, when he had devoted two hundred pages to abusing life even more than the Éléonores and Albines.

"I've nothing left but my pencils," she said, on the edge of tears. "And if I discover that I've no talent, that my vision of things is impossible to communicate, what will I have left?"

"Forty or fifty years that will be peopled with other Éléonores."

"Shut up, I hate you."

For several hours, they had been wandering about Paris. They passed through a little square where some mothers were knitting and watching their children playing round them. A young woman, leaning over a pram, was making a long, lisping sound to a little human larva. In the public gardens, mothers flaunted their silliness more shamelessly than ever in the sunshine.

Claude did not resist the impulse to make her lose her temper.

"Get married," he jeered. "Produce children."

"I'd rather give birth to a thousand herds of elephants!"

They crossed the cemetery of Père-Lachaise. There, too, mothers were taking their infants for walks without bothering about the dead. Where could one escape from them?

Twilight was falling. In the thick dusk, the houses seemed skeletal. In spite of the slowly vanishing daylight time stood still, fixed for ever, paralysed. The babies would always be babies, they would never grow up; the dead would always be dead. Claude and Sylvie wandered on, possessed by their demon, the refusal of life, without any thought of dinner, or of stopping. They were walking, in a fleeting eternity, beside the black water of the Saint Martin canal.

"It's beautiful, this hour of day," Sylvie murmured in spite of herself. "I'd like to be able to go on walking in it for ever, to live in that last light on the roof-tops."

But one cannot build one's life on the love of streets and twilight. The night soon engulfed her again.

"I'm going to drown myself," she thought, "relive my whole life, brutally resurrected in one final flash, then never hear it mentioned again. To die and to forget that one is dead, that there was ever such a thing as life. When one's alive, one can't forget that one's alive."

"Suppose we jump, Claude? Look how the water glitters."

"I don't like swimming, still less diving."

She was standing on the edge of the canal and

132

staring at it, hesitating. He realised that she was not joking.

"I shall die alone," he said softly. "You have no reason to escape the years you have still to live be-cause *you* believe in God."

She shrugged her shoulders.

"If I believed in God, I shouldn't want to kill my-self because Éléonore prefers him to me."

"If you didn't believe in him, you wouldn't have loved Éléonore. She'd have appeared to you as she probably is, a rigid, rather pathetic old maid. There are enough light women in the world, whether they're tarts or respectable bourgeoises. Why did you go and get infatuated with someone who's practically a nun?"

"It was really the architect I loved."

"The architect in love with God to the point of forgetting all about architecture. And, if I've under-stood you right, even so you wouldn't have lost her if you yourself hadn't trembled before God."

They had begun to walk again. Sylvie lit a cigarette.

"I shall never know whether I really could have lured Éléonore back to life or whether I dreamt it. All I know is that I shan't have the courage to go on living without ever hearing of her again."

She had spoken these words in a tone of such con-viction that Claude was impressed by it. He seized Sylvie's hand and said slowly: "Death is no solution for anyone who believes in hell. Anyway, don't forget you believe just as much in your pencils and paintboxes. I promise you that you shall see Éléonore again. We've got mutual friends at the Beaux-Arts, I'll easily manage to persuade them to arrange a meeting for us. But forget that you want to die; your death would seem more absurd to me than my life."

"Why did you say just now, 'I shall die alone'?"

He hesitated, for a second.

"Because it's up to me to put my theories into practice. Suicide is only legitimate for someone who no longer admits that life has any possible justification. But I've set my heart on seeing you at my funeral!"

He said this so gaily that Sylvie attached no importance to it. All she retained of this conversation was a promise that restored all her zest for life: Claude was going to arrange for her to meet Julienne.

They had arrived in front of the little shed where first aid was given to the drowning. A man, sitting on a bollard, was polishing his boots.

"He must be a master-swimmer or a master-life-saver," whispered Claude. "We'll go and ask him what the job's like."

He went up to him and offered him a cigarette. The man made no bones about talking. The job, he confided to them, was a tough one. People threw themselves into the water with a marked preference, it seemed, for the depths of winter, with no consideration for the watchman on duty. He had fished them out at a temperature well below freezing-point at two o'clock in the morning. More often than not, when you'd rescued them, they insulted you.

"Why don't they throw themselves under a train?" he sighed. "Then they wouldn't get wet and we wouldn't either!"

Sylvie inwardly promised the unfortunate life-saver that she would never choose his canal to throw herself into.

The next day, she telephoned Albine. Claude's promise had worked a miracle; once again she wanted to see her friends, to eat chocolate truffles, to become a remarkable, if not famous, painter. For a brief moment, she even thought of getting in touch with François. He had ceased to give any signs of his existence, a fact which made him almost lovable. But she remembered he was suffering from marriage fever and decided not to expose herself to infection.

Albine came rushing round, trumpeting her joy.

"We're leaving in six weeks, Sylvie. And you're coming with us, aren't you?"

"What good would I be to you? I loathe camping and sleeping out-of-doors and living like a brigand. Anyway, in September, I'm going to pass the entrance exam for the Beaux-Arts. For the last ten days, I've been getting into training at the Académie de la Grande Chaumière. I'm very keen on it, and, funnily enough, I think my parents are keen on it, too. They'd give anything to see me really working at something, no matter what."

"Exploring isn't a lazy life."

"It's an adventure, but it doesn't appeal to me. I'm sorry, Albine, but I dreamed up this life for you. My own is quite different."

Albine took these words as a reproach and was annoyed.

"I've associated you for so long with everything I am, everything I long for and hope for. Now you're deserting me. That's how *I* see your refusal to come."

"You wouldn't by any chance be an egoist, Albine dear? What would you say if I implored you to come to the Beaux-Arts with me?"

Sylvie suddenly turned her head away. She had reminded herself that this was what she had implored Julienne.

"You can't really associate yourself with someone else's life, even if it's the life of people you love," she went on sadly. "I've arranged to meet Claude at the Racine in a few minutes. Will you come with me?"

"Why not?" said Albine, in an almost aggressive tone. "You know I'm very fond of him. I haven't got over making him run away to the country."

They made their way to the Racine on foot. Both of them had the feeling that they were living through the last of their adolescence and that they only had a few days left, a very short distance to go before they reached the parting of the ways.

Claude welcomed Albine without the slightest embarrassment. Sylvie was amazed at his serenity and, for a moment, envied it. She herself was in a fever, no longer able to think of anything but Julienne.

"Have you managed to get in touch with your friends at the Beaux-Arts?" she demanded at once, in a shaky voice.

"Yes, dear impatient one. They're giving a cock-tail party in a week's time in honour of the twentieth anniversary of their wedding, and they're fully pre-pared to write Éléonore a highly moving letter that will force her to come."

"She won't come."

"I'm the one who's going to write the letter."

"In that case, she probably will come."

"How much stronger and steadier friendship is than love," thought Sylvie. "Albine and Claude are meeting again as if it were the most natural thing in the world, because Claude's love hasn't destroyed his friendship. And Claude comes to my help with-out any shilly-shallying, whereas Julienne hasn't hesitated to put up a wall between us without caring to know whether or not I might get smashed against it. But what gives them stability is affection, not passion. I want to see Julienne again."

137

While Sylvie was cherishing the frail hope, Claude was jeering affectionately at Albine's plans.

"It's dangerous to go trotting round the globe. You end up by realising that you're going round and round in circles."

"You only go round and round in circles by sticking inside yourself. That's what you're doing," Albine fumed.

He smiled. "You're right. It would be no good my rushing all over Persia and the Indies and Burma, I wouldn't be able to forget that the world is hopelessly round and that I'm only brushing its surface. That's enough of profound thoughts—will you come to the cocktail party where Julienne, I mean Éléonore, will at last be revealed to us?"

"Curiosity isn't one of my hobbies."

"Suppose I ask you to come—for my sake?"

"I'll come."

The trio was re-forming, more irreplaceable, more threatened than ever. Yet Sylvie was conscious of a small but real warmth in her heart that no love could ever give her.

The euphoria of that evening spent to the accompaniment of music and alcohol was so pleasant that, when she was back home, it seemed impossible not to overwhelm Julienne with it. She was going to dissipate all misunderstandings, sweep away all reservations by sheer force of honesty and affection. She felt ready to make any concession, any sacrifice provided she could make her best feelings, her best self triumph in the end.

"Dear Julienne,

You forbid me to write to you. It would be kinder to forbid me to breathe. I have sent you a thousand letters at a time when I was only thinking of myself though I honestly believed I was worrying about you. Tonight I would like to remember, all the time, what makes your whole world. It has triumphed over me, it triumphs in you. God must be served first, you used to say. I cannot fight against Him. But does that make us enemies? I am not on the devil's side.

Forgive me if I hate the average nun, and the average notion of the deity. All the same, for years and years, ever since I became conscious of myself, everything in me aspires towards an orthodoxy, something one could strive towards, something one accepts without question, something fundamentally different from my own experience—the shock of a bright light in darkness, the clear vision of excellence after mediocrity.

The light must inevitably exist somewhere, just as much, and more authoritatively, than the darkness. If the blind man learnt that night ruled the world, his blindness would become, for him, the end of the world. I am not even blind.

Julienne, I do not know whether what you prefer to me is heaven or a timid retreat from the world. For me you were the light, you lived by it at the Beaux-Arts, long before going off to discover it at Sainte-Thérèse. I firmly believe that, just as a day includes sunshine and night, we carry darkness and light inside us. And we oscillate between the two at the mercy of some unknown tide. But, for me, you are all sunshine, sunshine of my love, sunshine of your sacrificed youth, sunshine of your love, unquestionably God. Therefore, I can only approach Him through you. Because, in my eyes, you embody Him in life, it hurts me to see you leaving life. But the truth is that this light means that you are more than life, more than my life.

Do you want me to die of it?

Sylvie."

Two days later she received her letter back unopened and inscribed with the words: *"Return to sender."* She recognised the handwriting of Mother Marie-Sainte-Cécile.

When life has lost all meaning, all orientation, it leaves you drifting at random. Sylvie went to the Grande Chaumière, to Albine's home, to her own, to Claude's, like a sleep-walker. She dared not rejoice in her approaching, hypothetical meeting with Julienne. Henceforth an entire Order, an entire religion raised up a wall between them. Mother Marie-Sainte-Cécile was its ruthless sentry.

13th July.

Three o'clock in the morning. A morning still all submerged in night. In the dark, my heart beats in great hammer-strokes, another clock among the clocks of the neighbourhood. Slowly, but surely, time is pounding me to death. Every minute takes me further from Julienne. Yet in three days' time I shall see her. She has accepted the invitation worded by Claude. But we shall meet again on either side of a pit that nothing can ever fill in again. Will she flee at the sight of me, as if I had cloven hooves? Yet my love had no weapons at all . . . I even believe it was perfectly pure. But she cannot forgive me for having wanted to lure her back to secular life and she has transformed what, for me, was a source of life into an evil spell. I do not acknowledge her right to thrust me down into hell. What abominable prudence makes her have no hesitation in turning me into her bad angel? In becoming Saint-Touch-me-not in a convent because of me? Had I really so much power that I was a danger to her soul?

I would like to sleep, but I am too wretched. And I know, with a terrifying certainty, that, in three days' time, I shall be suffering even more.

When Sylvie entered the studio belonging to Patrice and Geneviève Montezel, her first impression was one of amazement. Everything in it appeared to be designed for admiration and nothing whatever for comfort. The Montezels seemed to have even more passion for plants than for pictures and sculpture. This studio resembled a virgin forest. Roots, tree trunks and a host of rare plants covered the walls or stood on pedestals. Hardly a flower was visible. Erudite labels adorned the pots and sometimes appeared stuck in places where the plants, scattered all over the flat and even in the bathroom, ought to have been.

Claude introduced Albine and Sylvie to the few people who had already arrived. Sylvie had no desire to talk. She had definitely come for the sole purpose of seeing Julienne and she had to make a great effort to reply to the mistress of the house and even more to listen to what the latter was saying to her. Nevertheless, inwardly fascinated as she was by her despair, it was not long before she became aware of the charm of the happiness that emanated from Geneviève Montezel. She even discovered that she was beautiful. She had a charming face and, though she looked her age, she carried her forty years with incomparable, almost childlike grace. Imperceptible tiny wrinkles gave that childish face a surprising maturity and, though they really were imperceptible, they gave her a look that was hard to describe, a suggestion of something perishable.

Was she conscious of Sylvie's unhappiness? Did she want to distract her from it, or was it simply a spontaneous sympathy that induced her to show her the statue she had finished that very afternoon? She took her away from the other guests and Sylvie found herself gazing at the headless body of a woman whose beauty derived neither from perfection of shape nor grace of attitude. At eighteen or twenty, no woman would have accepted that belly, those distorted shoulders without cursing nature. Yet the subject was a very young, mysteriously beautiful woman. The slim muscular legs and the taut thighs were those of a girl. The hips and the shy passion conveyed in their forward thrust expressed all the vital urge of adolescence. But the upper part of the body swerved away. For the first time, Sylvie saw the whole of a personality revealed in an eager movement of the loins, a shrinking recoil of the shoulders. A profound sympathy attracted her to that person with no face, to that arrogant pelvis, that despairing breast. "She is like me," she thought. "She wants to live, but she cannot succeed."

The absence of the head and arms only made the life imprisoned in those eloquent muscles all the more touching, all the more fleeting, in spite of the stability of the wood and the grandeur of the form

cut off by deliberate design at the neck and fore-
arms. If it brought to mind the broken marbles of
antiquity, this was only because it made one all the
more conscious that this was no incomplete work,
mutilated by time, of which only a fragment remains,
but a body sufficient unto itself, a finished statue.

"I'd like to see you work," Sylvie stammered out.
"You're a genius."

Geneviève broke into a joyous, friendly laugh.

"You scare me with your big words. Anyway, I'd
find it awfully embarrassing to work with someone
looking on. But we'll certainly see each other again.
I shall insist on it."

They went back to the party. As they were making
their way to the buffet, Geneviève saw Sylvie
abruptly stop, her face distorted. Julienne Blessner,
seeing her suddenly appear, had turned her back on
her. She had gone up to one of the green plants and
seemed to be studying it with so much attention that
she had practically buried her face in it.

"I don't want anyone to see me go pale, I don't
want to faint," Sylvie muttered to herself idiotically.

"It's probably the heat," said Geneviève in a
worried voice. "I'll tell them to open the window."

But she was staring at Sylvie as if she had guessed
that the heat had nothing to do with this agitation.

Sylvie thanked her, hardly knowing what she said,
and marched up to Julienne.

"I've forgotten you for ten whole minutes," she

said wildly. "That hasn't happened to me for a long time."

Julienne turned round, taken aback.

"You've made up your mind I'm the devil," Sylvie went on in a feverish, smothered voice. "You think you'll gain paradise at my expense, but you're wrong. You're definitely committing a sin by sacrificing me on the altar of your bigotry. We're told we must love our neighbour as ourselves. I am your neighbour and yet you don't hesitate to destroy me."

"You're drunk."

"Not yet," said Sylvie, snatching up a large glass of whisky.

Julienne remained silent, as if walled up in her dumbness. Sylvie drank, keeping her eyes fixed on her.

"She isn't made-up, she's wearing her hair in a bun, she doesn't smile. I've fallen in love with a scarecrow. But she's gone off to conquer heaven without me. I'm fighting against the angels, I'm drinking and I'm damning myself. I'm losing my soul through her, because of her."

Sylvie grabbed another glass of whisky and swallowed it in one gulp.

"No, through her, but because of myself. I wouldn't crave for heaven in someone else if there were any glimmer of it in me."

Julienne emptied her glass of orangeade and made an effort to smile.

145

"One has to accept suffering," she said in a low voice. "You don't know how to accept. That is why suffering destroys you."

Sylvie was on her third, then her fourth whisky.

"I'll never accept. If God loves men, it can't be at such a price."

"Do you imagine that I'm not paying it myself? But you prefer yourself to Him and that can only lead to despair. I want to be able to give you what you want from me, I can only do it by submitting myself to the demands of my faith. You will realise one day that we can only love in God, that there is no other good."

Sylvie felt suffocated with rage and despair.

"What I realise at this moment is that your God is a monster. I'm perfectly willing to sacrifice my pleasure, even my life to him, but not my sense of humour. Because that's the only part of me that's stimulated by your sermons. I thought I loved an angel, and it turns into a dreary little nun. Run along and join your female dragoons, complete with moustaches. You'll find plenty of other Sylvies to follow in your footsteps. I prefer hell to a treacle heaven. We love with our heart, with our blood, with every fibre in our being. What is the soul except that living structure? I loved you. No cardboard image will ever inspire in me one particle of that fervour. I loved you as I loved myself. That is the second commandment, like unto the first."

"You're blaspheming."

"I don't care a bloody damn."

Why had Albine suddenly appeared from nowhere, with a face like a policeman? She dragged Sylvie, hiccuping violently, away to the bathroom.

"I'm spewing up God," enunciated Sylvie, bent double over the wash-basin.

Soon afterwards, Sylvie found herself on a bed, with Geneviève Montezel, Claude and Albine whispering beside her.

"We'd better take her home," suggested Claude. "The air will do her good."

"Sleep will do her even more," said Geneviève. "Leave her with me till tomorrow."

"She's got parents," began Albine.

"My husband will see her home; he's very tactful. He'll get her off the smacking she deserves," said Geneviève, laughing.

Sylvie heard no more. She was fast asleep.

Julienne was saying good-bye to the considerable number of friends she had met again that night, and whom she thought she was leaving behind for ever, when Claude planted himself squarely in front of her.

"I want to talk to you," he said firmly. "My cousin isn't the only person who's obsessed by you."

"What do you mean?"

"I'll explain if you'll come and sit down with me for a minute."

Hypnotised, Julienne sat down. Couples had begun to dance to a gramophone.

"I bet you loathe dancing," said Claude, in a decidedly disagreeable voice.

Julienne did not reply.

"I wonder what horror or what nostalgia our world can inspire in anyone who violently turns away from it. However, it isn't a press interview I propose to inflict on you, forgive me. I'm extremely fond of Sylvie and I resent the confusion you're throwing her mind into, even more than her feelings. I saw you enter this studio and I realised that your prestige in her eyes . . . and in mine"—Claude averted his head—"comes from the fact that what is a living reality to you is nothing to us but lumber left over from an outworn past. Shall I admit I envy you as the Bohemian envies the civil servant, the adventurer envies the wholesaler? You live with a guarantee."

Claude produced a packet of cigarettes and offered one to Julienne, convinced she would refuse it. She accepted it.

"You've no need of me to discover the world of certainties," she said quietly.

"How do you know? I remember that before she went to Sainte-Thérèse, Sylvie rejected everything, as I do. Ever since you've been living in her, God has been battering at us."

"And is that why I obsess you?"

148

Julienne's tone was resolutely light and sarcastic. Claude looked her straight in the eyes.

"Yes," he said simply.

Claude regretted that Julienne did not strike him as being remotely desirable.

"And yet," he went on, "how well I understand why most people don't believe in God and refuse to discuss the subject. It seems to them absurd and, above all, ineffably boring. When I'm in really good health, I never want to talk about God. He doesn't interest me. But once you begin to suffer and clutch your belly, he's got you by the guts. He explodes in you."

"I've never loved God more than in my times of greatest happiness."

"Lucky you! You must certainly have a soul. Personally, I regard all those people who have one, and who talk about it, with amazement and curiosity. What's more, I'd like to point out to you that people say of someone 'he's got a beautiful soul' as one might say 'she has red hair'. I cannot see that one is any more responsible for one's soul, one's good qualities, one's defects than for one's face or one's figure. We rightly admire a person who is good or generous or gay just as we admire beauty or virtue, because they exist, not because they are a merit."

"Certainly our bodies are given to us, but we are responsible for them for life."

"And suppose they don't suit us? Albine de

149

Cêtres, whom you met just now, wanted to be a sailor; now she's an explorer. But, at sixteen, I wanted to turn the world upside-down, so how do you expect me to live without trampling my life underfoot? I'd like to see a man three centuries old, or a man with no arms and legs, come into this room. I suppose you'd tell me that they were responsible for their bodies."

"They are. You haven't turned the world upside-down, but you are responsible for yourself, Claude Ceyvenole."

"I've dreamed of dancing my life."

"Very well, then, dance!"

Julienne had risen to her feet. Claude leapt up from his chair and took her at her word. A tango was flowing from the gramophone. Dazed, Mademoiselle Blessner let herself be swept into it.

"I annoy you prodigiously because I'm the wolf prowling round the sheepfold," whispered Claude, doing his utmost to give their swaying hips an insidious languor. "I'd like to avenge my cousin. She set off in pursuit of you as if she were seeking the Holy Grail, and you've betrayed her."

"Perhaps what you call my betrayal will remind her that God brooks no rival. I am tired of dividing myself between this studio and Sainte-Thérèse, Sylvie and my duty, your tangos and my Gregorian chants. From the fact that you talk about it so vehemently, I imagine that you haven't always looked on religion as worn-out rubbish?"

The tango had ended and they returned to the sofa.

"One can't rape God," sighed Claude. "I only encountered him once, at seventeen. Later on, he always appeared to me absurdly disguised. But I can still remember that summer morning when I was sitting, in pyjamas, eating my bread-and-butter. A bee was flying between me and the sky and the sun came in through the wide-open bay-window.

"I am a Protestant. I had just come to the end of my religious instruction and I had been hesitating for a week about formally entering my Church by surrendering myself to the ceremony of First Communion. The bee was circling over the jam, there was so much sweetness, so much laziness in the air that I felt ready for every kind of surrender. Did I dream it or did tongues of fire begin to rain on my table? I felt surrounded by love, invaded by God. But the bee kept on buzzing. It was that bee that gave me the strength to shake myself, to escape from this madness. I said 'no' in a loud, clear voice. 'Bee, you are nothing but a bee; sun, you warm me, but you are not fire. At least not here.' I said no, and, ever since I've kept on asking myself whether that wasn't what you call the sin against the Holy Ghost."

"That's childishness. You were afraid of surrendering to the warmth of the sun."

"But the thing that happened inside me, I didn't dream that. I said no out of fear of ridicule, and because I wanted to infuriate my parents by refusing to go to Communion. I've often been conscious of bees and sunshine again but never of that mysterious warmth. You no doubt possess it all day and every day and you splash us with it."

"I only possess it on very rare occasions. But, surely, a memory as intense as that should be enough to save you from despair."

"Ah, but what about laughter? I've never been more staggered than the day I discovered the Catholic Church makes despair an unforgivable sin. Laughter, or rather derision, locks you up in it. No bee, no sun can ever free you from it then. It's your great strength, to have transformed the evil, and what causes the evil, into a sin and make us bear the responsibility for it."

"A little humility is all you need to free you from that evil."

"I merely refuse to let myself thank heaven for it. I don't know whether I've sinned against the Holy Ghost but I do claim to be still capable of distinguishing a cabbage from an orange and an absurdity from a truth. You are living through your renunciation, I am dying through my refusal, but, apart from a few symbols, the funerals will be the same."

"When you have resolutely turned your back on

this world, you possess the fullness of life. And no funeral can deprive you of it."

She reddened slightly. What she was about to say seemed difficult to bring out to the rhythm of a rumba, among people who were all a little drunk. But she articulated the words clearly, though her voice was hardly more than a whisper:

"I will pray for you. And for Sylvie."

Claude thanked her coldly. Seeing Albine approaching, rather hesitantly, he leapt to his feet with one bound.

"This rumba's worth all the *requiems* in the world. Albine my sweet, we haven't had a chance to have a good laugh together tonight. Come and dance and at least give me a little smile."

When Sylvie woke up, the dust was dancing in the sunlight that came in through the wide-open window. Geneviève brought her a big bowl of black coffee and two rusks and sat down on the edge of the bed.

"I've got a daughter who's your age and who behaves even worse than you do," she said gaily. "But she doesn't suffer from metaphysical drunkenness."

Sylvie drank her coffee without answering. "I ought to apologise to her," she thought, "but I don't feel like talking."

Patrice Montezel came in, in his turn, carrying his breakfast in one hand and holding a cigarette in the other. He was wearing pale green pyjamas that dazzled Sylvie. Her own father did not go in for elegant nightwear.

"It's no day for work. It belongs to the summer holidays, it's as blue as the Côte d'Azur," he sighed. "Paris is absurd in this sunshine."

"What are you planning to do this summer, Sylvie?"

"I had been thinking of working, preparing for my entrance exam to the Beaux-Arts, but now I don't know," said Sylvie peevishly.

Nothing was possible any longer. Neither sunshine nor holidays nor work. There was nothing left to her but despair. How often she had given that name to troubles that could be cured, to mere frustrations of hope, to postponements of happiness or pleasure, or even simply to boredom. That morning, the dawn had risen on the total absence of what, for a whole year, had been the substance of her life. The emptiness that stretched in front of her was bottomless and endless.

The Montezels' laughter rang out in that emptiness like a ridiculous challenge. Geneviève was looking at her insistently. Sylvie blushed. She suddenly realised that there is a certain discourtesy in being unhappy.

"I've no longer the least idea whether I ought to work or to give myself up to debauchery," she said, with a slightly forced smile and in a slightly forced voice. "I think I've a gift for both."

She had, after all, to say something.

"In that case, it's time you learnt how to drink," said Patrice. "We'll give you some lessons. You can tour the bars with my daughter when she gets back from England."

"I suppose I ought to ask them what this daughter's like," thought Sylvie, bad-temperedly. "She can be a dwarf, bandy-legged or a raving beauty for all I care. I'm not interested." She opened her mouth without any idea what she was going to say.

"When is she coming back?" she heard herself ask.

No one answered her. Geneviève had gone to fetch the coffee-pot and was filling the bottom of the bowl with coffee-grounds.

"I'm extremely curious," she said, with a dreamy expression that filled Sylvie with amazement. "I want to solve your mystery."

"Either she's cracked or she's a fool," thought Sylvie, in dismay. "And yet she's a great artist. Perhaps that gives her the power to see into people while she's playing this ridiculous game."

"Each of you turn your bowl upside down," ordered Geneviève.

Patrice obeyed, then bent over Sylvie's bowl, encouraging her to do the same.

155

"Darkness and light," Geneviève declared in a calm, deliberate voice when Sylvie had uncovered the coffee that had fallen on her plate. "Your character, your life, your thoughts are always brilliant light or intense darkness. All one, all the other, very rarely both.

"My grandmother was Russian," she explained suddenly. "She had a gift. I've inherited a little of it. At this moment, you have all this blackness you see there, in the middle of the plate, to go through. And, if I'm interpreting it right, you drink to give yourself the strength to get through it."

"There's no need to be a witch to discover anything as blatantly obvious as that!" exclaimed Sylvie. "I'm sure your daughter drinks with the utmost elegance; you've been able to observe that I don't. I've no idea what I told you last night when you were so kindly looking after what remained of me, but however ill I may have been, that doesn't stop me from looking on alcohol just as much as ever as a magic, even soul-saving, drink."

"You're talking more sense than you realise," Patrice declared with amusement. "That's exactly why most religions have taken it into consideration, whether they forbid it, like Islam, or whether, on the contrary, they make it the key to their mysteries, as Christianity has done of the red wine of the Eucharist. And as the Dionysian and Zoroastrian sects, to

156

mention only a couple, have also done with intoxicating drinks."

Sylvie gave him a warm smile.

"I'm convinced that most drunkards are mystics. But the tiresome thing about drinking is that the intoxication so soon passes off, even if you've swallowed the absolute in your third glass. And the morning after, you're back in time again and everything is arid. When evening comes, you've got to drink again to find eternity for a few hours. It's to be found in churches, too. But how can you discover it there if you don't have spiritual grace?"

"I'm the last person to be able to tell you," Geneviève said pacing up and down the room. "You strike me as remarkably serious for 'the morning after the night before'."

Sylvie blushed again. She asked to be allowed to get dressed and go home.

"Patrice will come with you."

"I'd like to take a short walk by myself. If you really want to spare me the paternal wrath, all you need do is telephone my home a little after mid-day and say that you kept me overnight because I'd missed the last train and we couldn't find a taxi. I'll arrive half an hour later and they'll never suspect a thing."

"What would you do if you had strict parents?"

"Desert them," answered Sylvie, with a smile.

When she found herself out in the street, she felt a kind of relief at being able to be sad with impunity.

All the rest of her life, would public gardens with their benches and gravel paths be permeated with the happiness Julienne had given for those few days? She sat down on the bench where they had sat together. Then she began to laugh.

"Idiot!" she shouted loudly.

A passer-by turned round. She stared at him till he lowered his eyes.

Insidiously, rebellion began to rise in her.

"This love is bursting my heart! All right, let it! I'll fling myself into debauchery, *I'll* become a nun, too, and I'll open my veins. Then I'll paint and I'll drink till I shatter the windows, I'll grab people by the throat and I'll make them burst, like soap-bubbles. With one stroke of the brush! Only take away this garden! I don't want to have to endure this gravel, these flowers, this sky a moment longer. Give me torrents, rivers, oceans of alcohol! I'd swallow death itself to escape from this moment. No, I prefer alcohol. It kills the moment and doesn't kill you. But what a temptation to kill yourself simply and solely to be somewhere else!"

She emerged at a run into the Place du Palais-Royal, went into a café and swallowed a neat whisky.

"A hair of the dog, as the English say," she mumbled. It had the desired effect.

"I've got to see Claude, I absolutely must talk to Claude."

She jumped into a taxi and told the man to drive to the Rue des Beaux-Arts. She knocked very softly on her cousin's door so as not to wake him if he were asleep. But he opened it at once. He was unshaven and obviously had not been to bed that night.

"You reek of spirits," he growled. "I loathe that smell. Don't forget I hardly ever drink."

"That doesn't make you any healthier."

"I'd feel even worse if I did. Still, it's true that for ages not sleeping has been doing me more harm than your getting sloshed. Sorry, I don't feel like talking."

He sat down on the edge of his bed. Sylvie had never seen him so depressed.

"What's the matter, Claude?"

He shook his head.

"Perhaps Éléonore's right. At least, if one wants to live. I'm still like those Carthusians who contemplate a hollow skull for hours on end and never forget that they're going to die. But I don't believe in the promises of death any more than in the promises of life, so I'd throw myself into it without hope. You're alive. Never forget that there's nothing like a great despair to save one from despair. Now please go away and leave me alone, I'm exhausted."

Sylvie went away, not knowing what to do next.

"If I go home, I shall cry. Where *can* I go?" At a street corner, a chemist's sign caught her eye. A word

flared up in her mind: CORYDRANE. She remembered the jubilant lift two tablets of this drug,
supposed to be an anodyne, had given her when she
was preparing to fail brilliantly in the Baccalaureate.

She bought a tube of it, asked for a glass of
water, and furtively swallowed half the tablets.
Then she started walking again. After a few minutes, an unusual warmth ran all over her, her
temples began to throb and a strange sense of exaltation made her quicken her step. It was at once
disquieting and delicious; a few pills had been enough
to abolish her misery and the impossibility of
everything and to give her a sense of eternity, a
marvellous conviction that never again would she
have to eat (except at a feast) or sleep or blow her nose,
that she possessed everything, that her cup of joy
was full to the brim.

"To hell with Julienne and her pieties!
Claude, you ought to come and play with me. If
you knew how to play you'd forget your dried-up
skulls!"

But play at what?

She stopped, disconcerted, then decided to walk on
the opposite pavement. As she was crossing the road,
a passing car brushed the edge of the cape Geneviève
Montezel had thrown over her shoulders. She turned
round, at first indignant, then suddenly enraptured.

"You would, would you? Right! I've always dreamt of being a bullfighter. Why deny myself the pleasure now that a thousand mechanical bulls are bellowing and about to hurl themselves on me?"

She undid the cape, spread out one fold, and, in spite of furious blasts from motor-horns, flung it over the nostrils of the Citroëns and Renaults and Peugeots that brushed past her at full speed, much to the alarm of their drivers.

"Bloody fool!" yelled an old gentleman on the pavement.

But she continued to advance without any fear, right in the middle of the road, flourishing her "muleta". A mist was softening the sky, the sun threw a halo round the trees. Was happiness going to triumph? It seemed even more tenuous than the mist. Suddenly, a flash of lightning struck her to the ground. She heard the blast of a policeman's whistle, saw the nickel-plated bumpers of a car above her head. What was the point of happiness? The sky, the houses, the passers-by and the street toppled over and vanished.

She woke up as if she were dreaming. In her mind she was drawing a picture of the Palais-Royal, the joys and miseries of the past. When she opened her eyes, she saw an oblong room with pale walls,

fat women in white overalls, a row of beds from
which came the sound of sighs. She uttered a string
of incoherent words. A nurse came up to her
bed:

"The doctor will examine you very soon. He's just
been called off to an urgent case."

"Get patient number seven ready," said a man's
voice. "She's being amputated at six o'clock."

She shut her eyes again. Life, that was yesterday.
What was she doing here?

Someone uncovered her.

"Severe concussion and she's lost a lot of blood,"
said the house-surgeon. "Is she delirious? Give her a
sedative."

She quietened down, but refused to sleep. The
hours went by. Far away, right at the end of a long
passage, there was death or recovery. Death, lying in
wait insidiously, would ambush her now and
again, then turn away, abandoning the body that
could still recover. Had it got to go on living, to keep
driving on this creature who had survived her and
in whom, nevertheless, she had to recognise
herself?

At the far end of the ward, an old man was groan-
ing. It sounded like some barbarous chant. At intervals, screams came from the adjoining ward. The
woman in the bed next to Sylvie's was chanting.

"I'm better! The doctor promised me I'll be well at

the end of the month," she cried triumphantly, without caring whether anyone was listening. She was beside herself with joy.

The nurse asked her for her name and address. She pretended not to know them.

"Another case of amnesia," sighed the fat woman. "Take things easy, your memory will come back."

"When I want it to," thought Sylvie, delighted at the success of her trickery.

They brought her her breakfast, then her lunch. She did not touch either. To deceive the nurses, she swapped them for a voracious neighbour's empty plates.

"I won't eat, I won't sleep, I'm here to go to the utmost limits of myself. Food and sleep would weigh me down."

Her heavy loss of blood and lack of sleep and food put a marvellous liberating distance between her and the people around her, between her and everything that was not herself.

Two days and two nights went by. Her mind was growing keener from hour to hour. She had given almost the entire contents of her note-case to a ward-maid to obtain a bottle of whisky. When she felt on the point of fainting, she swallowed enough to revive her. But she neither ate nor slept.

On the third day, she could no longer feel the weight of her body and the walls seemed to be about to draw apart, like curtains. Why shouldn't they begin to speak? For a moment, she believed that there was nothing left to prevent her transfiguration.

"A sign, I must have a sign. God, if you exist, come in through this window, on this moonbeam, make the sign of the cross on my bed."

The following day dragged, less successful than the day before. Nevertheless, Sylvie confidently awaited the hour of visions. She imagined them so powerfully that in the end she saw them. But they were only frail shadows in the dusk.

Sylvie had only one hope left now—to fly away.

"Then perhaps I'll escape from Julienne, from my parents, from the fat nurse and, above all, from myself."

But, having no wings, she could only fly in thought. She tried to do so.

"By sheer force of concentration, I'm going to rise up, slip between the beds, melt away the ceiling and the walls."

She imagined her flight so vividly that she got out of bed, hardly knowing what she was doing. Reality overwhelmed her; she could not stand up on her legs; she collapsed, and the noise of her fall made the nurse on duty come running.